ANNAECY

MARILYNN VICENTE

ANNAECY

MARILYNN VICENTE

I would like to dedicate my novel to my writer friends who helped me along the way. Thank you.

AUTHOR'S NOTE

Thank you, for choosing to read my novel. This is a fun and adventurous story. But there are some trigger warnings along the way. Below is a guide to show what is found in ANNAECY.

Mild and non-graphic:

- Bullying.
- Ableism.
- Emotional abuse/emotionally abusive relationship.
- Violence.

Quite mild or only briefly mentioned include:

- Ageism.
- Death.
- Famine.
- Kidnapping.
- Needles.
- Arachnophobia.

- Pregnancy.
- Stalking.

-Brief references to global warming/climate change.

PROLOGUE

AN EXPLOSION BLASTED out of the earth's atmosphere, wiping out the satellites in its way. It created a heavy suction that pulled in the debris, guiding its path while traveling long and far into the empty abyss, eventually crashing into an untamed planet. This particular planet's atmosphere was catastrophic. It held a thunderous weather pattern and had an unstable environment in all aspects. It could destroy itself with numerous lightning strikes hitting large piles of debris.

A sign of life struggled to emerge out of the debris. Subtle movement could be seen as a detached robotic hand with attached wires inched its way out. Magnetic pieces flew out of the pile and latched themselves onto the robotic hand, building a robot structure. Parts of the motherboards created a memory box, computers rebooted software. Pieces of silicone attached to the facial structures and bodies. Lightning strikes jolted the robots to life and soon others were being formed, thus creating an artificially intelligent robot-human hybrid. Over time, the planet's gravitational pull grew stronger and wider, casting an invisible net and pulling heavier things into the planet's atmosphere.

They harnessed the power from within their planet for their own usage, built structures to control the weather, miscellaneous items and buildings, applying what the humans had taught them. This time they needed humans for their experiments to see if it all worked. They imagined getting revenge on the humans who had once experimented on them and then thrown them away.

Improving their technology, they started attracting human-made crafts and the humans inside them. Pointing their high-powered satellite beam, the AI were on high alert when space shuttles and tourist shuttles landed safely on their planet. They worked quickly and efficiently to remove the humans, including their children, that were on board. The medic AI sat them down and began connecting wires to their heads, like the humans had done to them back on Earth. After wiping out any memories of the humans' past lives back on Earth, they began implanting new memories: who their new families were, how they had arrived, and memories with each other. They put their personal belongings safe inside a storage. The AI managed to keep the humans alive, monitoring their health in capsules. Years turned into centuries. Their experiment on creating a planet safe for humans was now complete. They had made it livable, comfortable, and set breathable conditions for their test subjects. Soon enough the humans completed their stay inside the capsules. The AI were ready to release the humans into their new homes. The next challenge was to learn how to create barriers between them and the humans.

CHAPTER ONE
QUONDAM

BEFORE HEADING OUTSIDE, Adina brushed her long, lush brunette hair, tied it into a perfect bun and threw her fedora on. The warmth beamed down on her face but there was a slight breeze that helped cool her down. It was a particularly heavy workload that day, but her sister, Wilhelmina, her younger niece, Estonia, and her mother, Sophia, made it all work. They tended to the livestock, adding fresh bedding to the cows, pigs and chickens.

The soil around here was rich and full of minerals, setting a perfect condition for growing crops, which made harvesting them an everyday job. Adina and Wilhelmina usually helped each other collect the well water and fill the in-ground water reservoirs back up. Although it was a tough job, they made a great team.

The winds around them gradually started picking up the loose dirt that lined the ground around the crops. Soon enough the dirt was everywhere, blowing in their faces. It hindered their ability to see and they had to stop working on the farm. Adina heard someone crying, and the sound of coughing led her over to Estonia. She was standing by the barn doors. Holding onto her fedora, Adina grabbed Estonia's hand and raced back to the mansion to Sophia and Wilhelmina.

Adina and her mother threw their fedoras on the armchair right next to the front door. They gathered towels from the supply closet in the hallway and ran through the house, closing the curtains and covering the windows and doorways with rolled up towels to stop the dirt from entering their home.

Estonia screamed out that there was dirt inside her eyes. Adina headed into the bathroom with her, turned on the bathtub faucet and rinsed her face with a small toy bucket, rubbing the dirt off with a wet towel. She could've given Estonia a clean set of clothes or run the bath for her, but when Adina turned around, she had run away. After all, she was afraid of the frequent dust storms every time she visited. Adina understood her a bit more this time. This particular dust storm was not like all the other ones Estonia had experienced. Her favorite hiding spot was behind the couch in the living room, right across from Adina's office. Estonia was twelve now but when she had been younger, they had often played peek-a-boo with her poking her head in and out of the couch. Adina figured that was why she loved being there.

She let Estonia be and didn't pry too much. Her leaving gave Adina enough time to head upstairs to her bedroom to bathe and change. Meanwhile, Wilhelmina ran upstairs to her room and began packing her suitcase instead. She was getting ready to leave for her trip. Leaving her daughter with her mother and sister was a fairly common occurrence and they didn't ask too many questions.

Adina's favorite part of living at home was all the wonderful memories. Staying there brought back those precious memories.

Their home was an elegant two-story house. Cream bricks lined the walls with large windows at the front. There were two large oak trees on both sides of the house as well as two outdoor lights, one near Adina's bedroom on the second story and another near the front door. Gardena bushes aligned the driveway, welcoming a pleasant aroma. The entranceway was met with white marble flooring and a curvy wrought iron stair railing. High vaulted ceilings, archways and a water fountain in the middle, four bathrooms, five bedrooms and a breathtaking closed-off garden where her mother's prize roses were gently nestled, protected and away from the dust storms.

Wilhelmina looked at herself in the mirror and began wondering if she was doing the right thing as a mother. She took the time to fix her messy blonde hair in a low updo, bathe with a washcloth to wash away the dirt, then changed into a simple white dress and applied red lipstick.

Sophia wasn't bothered by the dirt on her skin. Instead, she took a calmer approach, sitting down on the armchair right next to the front door. She rested her chin on her hand and looked out of the window. Before leaving, Wilhelmina tapped her mother on the shoulder to meet her in Adina's office.

Estonia was fed up with her mother leaving her with her grandmother often. No matter how much she tried to avoid her intuition, it kept nudging at her and she couldn't put those strong feelings aside; this time her mother leaving felt different. Regardless, she pouted and hid behind the couch. By this point, she wanted to avoid seeing her own mother, no matter what.

She heard a set of high heels and flat shoes and saw her

mother and grandmother walk into her aunt's office. They left the French doors wide open. Estonia knew she had an advantage when hiding behind the couch. She stuck her head out from the right side of the couch and was able to see her mother and grandmother talking loudly to each other and arguing.

Wilhelmina lowered her head and held her mother's hand. "I'm sorry, mother, but I won't be returning. I've met someone who doesn't like children. I know that you'll judge me, yet I must go. I've been searching for love and I feel like I've finally found it. But you must not tell Estonia. I wouldn't want her heart to become bitter and cold when she grows older."

Searching into her purse, Wilhelmina pulled out a ruby necklace. Sophia gasped. "Wilhelmina, where did you get this? This ruby necklace is fragile, and you know darn well that it is a valuable heirloom that has been in my family for many years. Did you steal it? To sell?"

Wilhelmina was ashamed of what she had done to her mother to such an extent that she felt guilty and avoided making eye contact with her. She put her hand up to cover her face and walked quickly out of the office. Estonia moved her head out of the way before her mother saw her. Sophia immediately became worried.

"Wait, Wilhelmina! Come back, darling. We can talk about this situation."

Wilhelmina said nothing and left without saying goodbye to her own daughter for one final time. After the winds died down, she closed the front door behind her. Estonia changed her mind and ran over to the door and banged on it. She didn't have the courage to run out of the house to face her mother and look her in the eyes to confront her about leaving forever. Instead, she ran over to the window but chose not to peer out through the lace curtains to see her mother getting into a taxi that was outside waiting for her. Estonia sniffled and covered her tears with her hand. Her grandmother heard her crying, and Estonia went over to her and hugged her.

Right after the taxi sped off, everyone else in town marched up towards the mansion and started banging at the front door. Their loud voices could be heard upstairs and the people screaming outside were scaring Estonia. Sophia became concerned and whisked her away from the noises. Adina opened the front door. She didn't understand why the towns-people were angry when they usually showed kindness towards her and her family. She tried calming everyone down.

"Please, I need everyone to be quiet," she spoke while motioning her hands. "You're scaring my niece and we can only solve this if everyone stays calm."

Kaiser cleared his throat. "Sorry, Adina, but we must know what is going on. Everyone knows the dust storms weren't this frequent or this strong before. All we want is someone of authority to tell us what is going on."

Adina shrugged her shoulders. She was as confused as they were. The townspeople always came to visit them when anything major happened. Their mayor, Nathaniel, didn't like to do anything and often went on vacation with his wife Savanna at the town's expense. He was only elected to office because of his corrupted father and his mother-in-law who was a prominent lawyer for his father. He had skipped town after it had been discovered that he was stealing the town's money. Even with that knowledge, the townspeople had still elected Nathaniel. The angry crowd had gathered all around the mayor's home and chanted, thinking that this time was going to be different. The mayor was out of town with his wife as usual, and they had left their most trusted employees, Lavinia and Edsel, in charge. They had both become frustrated by everyone being there and demanded them to leave.

With no answers from anyone, the townspeople were afraid the dust storms would make a return and intrude on their daily activities. They decided to board up and stay in their homes. Adina got Kaiser, his daughter Floria, and Sophia ready while Estonia stayed home. She was only twelve years old and Sophia felt like she was too distraught to help.

Everyone already looked up to Kaiser as he was a gentle giant. Besides having a strong physique, he was also helpful along with his lovely daughter. Floria's short stature could be deceiving, but she packed a punch. With their combined strength, they volunteered to help others in the community together with Adina and her mother. They helped with food deliveries, caring for the poor, harvesting the fields, calming down the livestock and assisting with veterinarian care.

Lavinia and Edsel lived a lavish lifestyle. They worked tirelessly with Nathaniel since they were more on his side. Kaiser and Floria still helped them out with whatever they needed, despite their differences.

Everyone emerged from their hibernation weeks after the dust storm and high winds had passed. Despite having no answers, the townspeople shrugged off the storm and soon enough forgot about all the good deeds that Kaiser, Floria, Adina and her family had done for them, and went about their day.

Three years had passed since Wilhelmina left. Sophia didn't want to confess it, but Estonia often reminded her of her mother. Sophia did often wonder about the whereabouts of her daughter, but as a mother she was truly disappointed in her. If Wilhelmina could go to the extent of abandoning her own daughter, then Sophia couldn't care less about her.

Sophia opened her armoire and spotted a lovely green dress hidden in the back. She smiled and put it on, then sat down on her vanity bench. Being a simple kind of woman, she only applied blush, fluffed her soft grey hair with her hands, applied red lipstick and put on her golden earrings, but nothing over the top. She heard Estonia run down the long hallway towards her bedroom.

"Grandma, look at me." Estonia smiled while twirling around in her yellow dress with patterns of white flowers on it. She looked cute with her curly blonde hair made into a ponytail, tied with a blue lace. "Look, Adina got me all ready to go to the market today."

Soon a loud, frantic knocking at the front door shattered their peaceful moment.

"I'll get it, Grandma."

Sophia intervened in Estonia wanting to open the front door and walked carefully down the stairs. It was Kaiser. He took off his straw hat when he saw Sophia and greeted her with a smile, hesitating a bit. "Sophia, I'm sorry for showing up like this at your door. Especially during this beautiful morning, on this particular day when you're heading to the market."

Sophia looked at him and smiled. "Why, hello there, Kaiser. Are you okay? Are you looking for Adina?"

That was when Estonia ran over to the door and hid behind Sophia. She was often afraid of seeing anyone from town. She wasn't used to them because she usually stayed inside during dust storms. She only ever went with Sophia to assist her on the weekends when she went to town. They often went to a nearby park to have lunch, walked around, then went to the market to buy their daily meals. Estonia would talk to Sophia about school. Adina went with her during the weekdays – after all, Estonia couldn't go lest she missed her studies. Sophia's main concern was that she didn't like talking to the townspeople and was often shy about it, but other than that, she talked to her family just fine.

Estonia was afraid of seeing Kaiser and it was a cause of concern for him.

"My apologies, sorry to have scared you with my loud knocking like that. Estonia, once again my apologies, miss. Are you doing okay now?"

Estonia nodded her head yes. Sophia took Estonia by the hand and smiled again at him. "Have a great day, Kaiser, and greet Floria for me."

Estonia turned around to smile at him and to wave goodbye.

Adina looked concerned. "Kaiser, what is wrong?"

Kaiser paced back and forth. "Sorry for knocking on your door like this, but you must come to the mayor's house. My daughter told me that she saw a new visitor there and that he didn't look too kind."

Kaiser carefully held Adina's hand to help her down the step and they walked over to Nathaniel's house.

There was a tall tree in the front yard of the mayor's house. Adina could barely get a glimpse past it at this stranger. When he moved his head, she caught a sight of him. She was mesmerized by how he carried himself when he talked to Nathaniel. Then she was taken aback by how handsome he was, which surprised her the most.

Kaiser didn't like the way she looked at the stranger, being a father himself. He felt like the stranger had bad intentions since he was talking to the mayor. Nothing good came from talking to the mayor.

"Adina, I am warning you. Do not fall in love with this man. He looks cruel, and I see you as my own daughter. All I want is for you to be careful, and knowing your mother, she wouldn't approve either."

Adina heard Kaiser talking but didn't register a word he said to her.

Around town, the stranger analyzed Adina everywhere she went. He mainly focused his gaze on her at the town square, admiring her every move. He had instantly noticed her and couldn't take his eyes off her extraordinarily beautiful personality. He was blown away by her kindness already, seeing how generous she was with everyone she saw at the town square, greeting them one by one and asking them how their day was going. He saw her lovely soul illuminated through her smile. She captured his heart right then and there. Now he saw why the whole town was in love with her – but then his illusion of her was dashed. He was stunned to find that she walked with a slight limp, and he didn't like that too much. He glared at her without her noticing him, but didn't let her limping get in the way of his real intentions. He remembered the mayor mentioning that she came from an extremely wealthy family and couldn't wait to get his hands on her money.

Adina saw him walking near her, but he covered his face with his hand and spun back around. He spotted her talking to a little old woman sitting on a bench and kept his distance from her for a bit, his eyes following her everywhere until she was completely alone. Then he lurked carefully until she didn't suspect him staring at her. But his strange behavior caught the attention of the others that were nearby. He wasn't trying to be obvious as he wanted to play his cards right in order to win her heart. After fixing his hair to the side, he made his move, swiftly approaching her while she said goodbye and smiled at a small child and her mother.

"Why, hello there, my name is Mortimort Montay. You must be Adina? I've heard wonderful things about you and seen you around town."

Upon meeting him, she instantly swooned over his handsomeness once again and his cute dimples when he smiled. She didn't think that the handsome stranger would even notice her due to her disability. Adina played with her braided hair and her cheeks flushed bright red when she saw him looking at her. He already knew she was clearly interested in him and he was excited about it. He wouldn't have to do much to serenade her. The sparkle in her eyes confirmed she was already his.

They both smiled and he asked her out on a date. Letting out a loud squeal, she gladly accepted. Adina was ecstatic and walked all the way back home.

Mortimort's smile faded away quickly. Everyone noticed his demeanor change hastily as his cold, dark stare returned the moment she left.

Adina rushed back home and went straight into her bedroom. She went through her wardrobe and threw all the dresses that she owned onto her bed. None of them seemed right for a romantic first date with the most handsome man in town.

Sophia saw her stressing out. "Adina, what has gotten into you?"

Adina smiled at her. "Mother, you wouldn't believe it, but that handsome stranger, Mortimort, asked me out on a date."

Adina spotted the red dress she had worn during the last ball. She danced and twirled, holding that dress in her hands. Her mother looked at her in the eyes and stopped her from dancing. "No, Adina, I do not approve of this. From the moment he arrived in this town, he has been trouble. Did you not go with Kaiser to see him talking with the mayor? Nothing good comes from talking to the mayor. Please listen to me and do not go out with him."

A month later, Mortimort and Adina got engaged. He manipulated her into thinking he was a kind person with a good soul and had good intentions. She was blinded by love and couldn't see that he was clearly using her. Less than a month after getting engaged, he bullied her constantly, calling her hideous. On their romantic evening walks, he would tease her disability in public and didn't care who was watching. Adina was embarrassed when she saw people she knew on the streets, whispering to each other, laughing at her and pointing fingers at her. In reality, all his mocking only made her stronger and didn't taint her heart one bit. Despite feeling embarrassed to go out with Mortimort, she mustered the courage to go for a walk with him. It was her only chance to get out of the house.

The whole town shifted into total darkness suddenly out of nowhere. Only the sound of heavy wind could be heard. Mortimort panicked and Adina heard his footsteps receding. She yelled out his name in the total darkness. People screaming and running all around her frightened her. The loud commotion made her want to curl up on the sidewalk.

The smell of burnt wood hit her nose first, then she saw a match light up a piece of plank. She felt safer when she saw two familiar faces appear in front of her. It was Kaiser and his daughter, Floria.

"That poor excuse for a man left you here all alone."

Adina broke down and tears streamed down her face. "I'm sorry I didn't listen to you, Kaiser. I also ignored my mother's warnings about him."

Floria cleared Adina's tears away and Kaiser carried her back towards the mansion. They saw trashcans on fire, providing light for the others to see. Kaiser put Adina down and everyone rushed over to bombard her with questions. They were talking all at once and she became overwhelmed. "Please, everyone calm down. I don't know what is going on either."

Kaiser intervened as well. "Everyone please treat Adina with respect. We are clueless of what is going on as much as everyone else here."

An eerie warning blared, stirring more fears among everyone. Strong rumbles could be felt underneath their feet. Red lights began to flash above them, making them look up at the sky. Two bright, circular lights hovered over them and steam filled the already pitch-dark sky, making the townspeople cough. Then the mysterious series of events disappeared, leaving them baffled, clueless and scratching their heads.

Outraged, the townspeople walked over to the mayor's house, but he wasn't home. The darkness did go away, the streetlights all turned on and the sun eventually returned the next morning, but the townspeople were left baffled and once again too afraid to leave their homes. Kaiser, Floria, Adina and Sophia went ahead and helped everyone out like they had done the last time an incident had occurred. When the townspeople felt like it was okay to come out of their homes, they returned to their daily activities, forgetting about the help they had received.

The next day, the air became suffocating and unbearable to

breathe. For what felt like hours, the conditions outside didn't change. Crops and trees soon withered away. Adina and her family worried as they knew the others needed help, but nothing could be done for them during this time. If that wasn't enough, the day after wasn't great, either, despite the heavy air going away. The dust storms came back. But the following week, everything went back to normal.

Mortimort snuck in through the backdoor in the middle of the night and made his way into his fiancé's bedroom while she slept. Estonia was woken up when she heard a loud crash from her aunt's room. Afraid and thinking the worst, she sprinted out of bed and saw Adina's lamp knocked over on the ground and it was still on. Then she saw movement inside the room and felt like something or someone was in there. Looking through the crack of the bedroom door, she spotted Mortimort getting something from his pocket. He pulled out a large copper syringe, he raised it up a little. Mortimort squeezed the bottom and a clear liquid began squirting out of the syringe. Estonia gasped and covered her mouth before he heard her. She didn't want him suspecting anyone was beside the doorway seeing what he was up to. Estonia grew curious and stayed.

Early in the morning, Mortimort woke up his fiancé. Adina was startled to see him after not hearing from him for weeks since he had abandoned her in the dark. She felt groggy, exhausted and sensed a headache coming. There was a sharp pain in her arm when she raised it.

"My arm hurts. What do you want, Mortimort? Do you think we are still going to get married even though you left me? And after all of your mocking me in public in front of everyone that knows me?"

He knew why her arm was hurting but said nothing, and he didn't care whether she wanted to get married or not. He kept his demeanor calm when he spoke to her. "Hurry, get dressed. Tell your mother and Estonia to get ready."

He became snappy towards her when she wouldn't hurry up.

"It's time for you to learn the truth. Do you know why I wanted to marry you? Do you want to know the real reason? It wasn't because of your kindness or your sweet heart. I actually don't like you and you make me sick. Your limp is what makes me sick. What I really want from you is your money, your lands and your mansion. Everything that you own will become mine."

Adina got out of bed to confront him. "Take it, I don't care. You can have it all, but leave my dignity alone. One thing you underestimated in me is that no matter what, I'll never stoop down to your level." She took off the ring that he had given her and threw it in his face.

Mortimort clicked his tongue. "You want to know how I won your heart? It wasn't difficult one bit. I won your heart over by being kind, and once I had you eating from my hand, I made fun of you because of your disability. Now I have ripped away what you adored the most. Wasn't it your love for me?"

He grabbed her face, kissing her hard and pushing her back down on the bed.

Adina was stunned to find out what his sick, cruel plan was all along. She should've listened to her mother and Kaiser, but she hadn't, and now her family had to pay the price. She got everyone ready, and when Mortimort went upstairs, Adina told Estonia to run out of the back door, head over to Kaiser and tell him what was going on. She at least knew that her niece would be safe there if she didn't return soon.

Adina held a blanket in her hands when she and her mother got into Mortimort's car. Fear arose in her when he drove them off the dirt road. Spotting a large mountain over the horizon, he yelled for them to get out of the car. They all got out and Adina dropped the blanket on the ground. Mortimort picked it up, held it out, and became furious. "What is this? Where is Estonia? You fool."

Amidst his anger, he tied Adina and her mother together with a rope. He got keys out from his pocket and unlocked a padlock on a large, wooden door, then yelled at them to go inside. Adina became furious and turned around to face him.

"Where are you taking us? Mortimort, can you at least take my mother home? After all, you want to harm me and not her. I already told you that you can have everything."

He pushed her waist while ignoring her. Sophia tried to calm her down. Walking further down in the pit of darkness, Adina and her mother both saw something green glowing. While they were distracted by the sight, Mortimort wasted no time and ran out of the cave, locking them inside.

They emerged from the mountains on Estonia's seventeenth birthday. Sophia couldn't wait to celebrate with her. Once they broke through the door, it was eleven o'clock at night. They ran all the way home. They thanked Floria and Kaiser for staying with Estonia all this time. They were confused as to why Adina and Sophia had been gone for so long,

"Estonia came to find me that day when Mortimort appeared and you told her to run. Floria and I came with weapons, ready to fight, but the house was empty with all the lights on. I checked every room alone while Estonia waited with Floria by the front door. We stayed here with her thinking that you'll return, but days turned into months, then years. I knew that it was my job to take care of Estonia like my own."

They thanked them for taking care of Estonia for years, but the two couldn't explain it in depth. They had no other choice but to shoo Kaiser and Floria out of their house and tell them that they would explain everything when Estonia turned eighteen. Saying goodbye to Floria and Kaiser gave them enough time to get cleaned up. Adina and Sophia then pretended to be asleep.

It was finally Estonia's eighteenth birthday party. Sophia decorated the house to her liking. The day had finally arrived and the ambience in the room felt uncomfortable to Estonia. Kaiser and Floria came over and they all gathered it was now time to gift Estonia the ruby necklace. Adina and Sophia took a deep breath, and after celebrating, headed into town to convince the townspeople to come live underground with them. Floria and Kaiser stared at them in discomfort.

With everyone gathered like they had done before, Adina and Sophia removed their sweaters. The townspeople's eyes grew wider. Panic arose among them. Everyone yelled at them, "Monsters! Monsters!"

They didn't understand what they were and they chanted for them to leave the town and began throwing rocks at them. Even though Kaiser and Floria were their friends, they were afraid of following them and didn't want to receive any backlash if they went underground with them. As much as they wanted to say goodbye, they had to stay behind. Adina and Sophia had to return to the mansion to take Estonia with them despite not wanting to go. By that point she had no other choice but to flee with her family underground.

CHAPTER TWO
ANNAECY

IT WAS NOW CR-70: The landscape changed around them, the soil was no longer usable, the rain ceased, causing the rich vegetation to die out. Annaecy soon became a deprived, gloomy, hollow, desiccate land. Throughout the trepidation of time, survival proved difficult to the families choosing to stay behind. Savanna was emotionally exhausted, dehydrated, hungry, frustrated, and she hadn't bathed in a while. Her clothing was tattered, rough to the touch and her tiny, fragile voice cracked hoarsely. "This is all your fault, Nathaniel. If you had listened to Adina and her family and fled with them, we wouldn't have to starve to death. Did you forget we made a huge promise to all of these families choosing to stay right here with us? Convinced everyone Adina and her mother were the actual monsters, and they shouldn't go with them? We should at least appreciate their commitment to us."

Nathaniel wasn't feeling too good even if he didn't complain as much as his wife. He had enough of Savanna tormenting him and bellowed in a deep but loud voice, "Savanna, haven't you noticed? We've survived here for three months, we can do it again."

His emotions overwhelmed him and his fists clenched. Savanna's hands moved to her hips, as if scolding a disappointing child. "Oh, right? But all the food we foraged for is nearly gone. Most of it is to keep the children from starving. And on top of that, the water reservoirs are nearly empty. Have you been outside yet? Go look for yourself, I want you to go outside, now! The town that once survived is now lying in decay, it's no longer what it used to be. Does your massive ego ignore everything? Pretend to ignore everything, even the lack of oxygen! We need supplies to thrive. Or are you going to continue to ignore that, as well?"

Nathaniel had enough of hearing his wife disapprove of him. Stepping closer to her but maintaining an arm's distance, he said sarcastically, "Then what is the gist? Tell me, Savanna. Does your plan consist of digging into the earth to try and reach them?"

Savanna felt desperate trying to reason with him. She gave up. There was no getting through to him. Her eyes grew heavy as she kneeled down. Tears slid down her cheeks, falling to the desolate dirt. "I'd have to cry an ocean just to dig a hole in this depleted land."

The townspeople emerged from the abandoned mansion that was covered in vegetation, furious, quashed by fear and uncertainty washing over them. The lack of oxygen weighing heavily on their minds, families became worrisome for their children's survival.

Not all hope was lost. The rhythm of lightning filled the sky and vibrations could be felt throughout the land. An eerie yet familiar sound of thunder soon followed. This remarkable news brought celebration. Nathaniel pulled Savanna towards him. He swept her hair behind her ear and looked deep into her eyes.

They no longer cared what differences had broken their relationship. All that mattered was having her in his arms. He leaned in, tenderly kissing her. Afterwards, they both smiled.

The lightning strikes increased in frequency, the thunder grew rapid and heavier, much more so than the storms the people in town remembered. The thunder foretold the turbulent clouds worsening above them. Small, black tendrils descended from the clouds, frightening the children as they clung onto their parents' legs. The adults' curiosity piqued and anticipation was building. The clouds promised rain, but sadly it was not rain. Instead, large amounts of black debris showered down, and they understood why the children were frightened. Smiles faded once they spotted how quickly the ashes began sticking to them and their tattered clothing.

Desperation set over them as they attempted to remove the ashes from their skin, growing irritated. It wasn't working. The parents wasted no time scooping up the children and descending back into the mansion.

The ashes falling from the sky stuck onto the roof, rapidly covering the windows and making it difficult to see outside. The ashes seeped in, eroding their way inside the mansion. Nothing could be done, unfortunately the ashes spread no matter how much they tried covering the floors with blankets. It was hopeless trying to stop it or make it go away. Soon enough, the whole town was engulfed in ashes, eventually giving in to its own demise.

After being completely covered in ashes, a burning sensation overwhelmed people's retinas and skin. The toxicity of the ashes seeped into their bloodstream, causing blindness.

All was not lost, eventually the ashes falling from the clouds stopped. The townspeople stumbled out from the mansion once again, unable to see what was in front of them. However, their sense of smell was enhanced, their skin felt gritty and scaly to the touch. They desperately wanted to communicate, but couldn't. What came from their mouths was not understandable.

Nathaniel felt he needed to become the leader. Touching people's hands carefully and leading them, he positioned them where he wanted them to stand next to each other. Forming a human chain, he walked forward and the rest soon followed.

The townspeople who had chosen not to go with Adina or Nathaniel stayed on the other side of Annaecy. They felt they were protected with Kaiser. Flabbergasted, they too anticipated the coming of the rain. They too saw the rhythm of lightning fill the sky, felt vibrations throughout the land, and the familiar sound of thunder followed. Seeing the frequent lightning in the sky was a cause for concern for them as well.

Kaiser grew curious. Why hadn't the rain come yet? Squinting his eyes towards the distance, he spotted small, black pieces falling on the other side of town. He walked over and extended his finger to catch the falling debris but received a surprise instead. He could physically feel an energy barrier separating both sides of Annaecy. Puzzling, he thought. Confusion welled after he felt a small jolt of electricity contacting his finger. He pulled away quickly due to the intense pain. The soothing and familiar sound of rain caressed his skin, causing a distraction from the pulsing, sharp pain infecting his finger. His heart became full, his smile radiant, and he ran excitedly over to the others to celebrate with everyone. But the celebration was premature; the small droplets changed into massive droplets, pouring down in an endless amount of rain. Soon enough, small puddles grew into lakes.

Edsel desperately approached Kaiser. "Kaiser! We must

seek higher ground. The water has risen to our homes, we are no longer safe here. Despite our differences, we must warn Nathaniel and the others."

Kaiser urged him to stop. "No, don't go! Don't go over there, it is not safe."

Edsel became aggravated. "I know you two have your differences, but I am not going to stand here and watch Nathaniel and his family as well as all the other families die because of the childish behavior between you two."

Before Kaiser could react, Edsel sprinted away, crossing to the other side. A strong force pulled him backwards and the lightning struck his arm, almost like an unseen force signaling a warning not to cross. Edsel moaned. The intense feeling from the jolt of lightning reverberated throughout his body as he hit the wet ground, increasing the great pain. Kaiser ran towards him, seeing Edsel's body convulsing. Not knowing what to do, he grabbed him by the arm and helped him up towards the mountain.

All the townspeople fled to higher land. They stood on the mountain, horrified, and watched their homes being swept away. The horror amplified when they realized the flood waters were only on their side of Annaecy. The small, black pieces falling on the other side eventually stopped, but an uneasiness swarmed over the people witnessing the others emerge from the mansion. Everyone stood in disbelief, speechless, and rubbed their eyes. The people coming out of the mansion were gray monsters. Their skin was coarse and lumpy, their facial features deformed and their eyelids swollen shut. Unsure of how to react, everyone on the other side wasted no time running away from the monsters and the rain, if it was possible.

They ran for miles until Kaiser saw freedom. Overjoyed to find someplace where it wasn't raining, the sun was shining and foliage could be seen for miles, they clasped hands, jumped and smiled at each other in the rain.

"Once we cross over, we will be out of this rain forever! All that we left behind can be rebuilt. Are you ready? I am," Kaiser pronounced eagerly.

Everyone took their first step out of Annaecy, and lightning bolts assailed them, one by one. The force knocked them to the ground, dragging them backwards. Defeat coursed through their bodies with the intense jolt, causing them to convulse as they hit the ground. In spite of it all, Kaiser pounded his fist against the ground, refusing to surrender, fuming and stubborn. He pushed himself up, then ran with all his might. Each step was greeted with a lightning strike, twice as powerful as the last. The impacts pushed him back even further, as if a punishment for attempting to cross each and every single time.

"Stop, Papa, stop! You're hurting yourself," cried Floria. She ran to her father. Her family joined them, offering their hands for strength. Kaiser was ashamed for thinking he was able to get through the barrier and realized it may have been there all along.

Floria stood in front of her father and spoke firmly, "We can all come out of this alive. You said we can always rebuild here. This rain won't keep us down if we all put our thinking skills together. We can control its flow, at least for a while. We can grow crops once again. Giving up isn't in our legacy, father, and that goes for everyone here."

Nathaniel felt guilty. He felt he couldn't be a good leader. He felt remorse for not being able to see or communicate with his wife. The soothing sound of rain rose to a crescendo, becoming hypnotizing with its rich, alluring voice. Confusion spread among the others, but why? Couldn't they feel it on themselves? It was worrisome. The rain sounded louder each time they moved towards it. Lightning bolts assaulted every one of them, one by one. The force of the strikes knocked them to the ground, dragging them backwards. They didn't feel the intense jolts of electricity coursing in their bodies as their thick, coarse skin acted as armor. For a while they refused to give up and forged ahead, stopping at nothing. Disillusioned, they believed they could somehow pass through.

An unknown force maintained, blocking them from going to the other side each time.

After a few strikes, some of them realized what was going on, feeling the familiar vibrations beneath their feet. They sensed the ground shake, and all they could do was wait for the thumping to get closer until they were able to push each other out of the way. They stomped their feet louder, vigorously, to show they wanted to stop trying to break through. All they were doing was punishing themselves.

They developed a way to converse using sounds, tapping on the dirt, learning to leave tracks in the dirt with their fingers and through touch. Nathaniel felt he could now become the leader and teach them to feel like family. He was ecstatic to be able to connect with Savanna again.

Given they were incapable of relying on their eyesight, what could they hunt for?

Becoming the only survivors in a barren land, they discovered they couldn't devour the rodents. They could only swallow anything after crushing it. Albeit it lacked taste, they knew it was the only way to survive.

Dehydration was soon upon them. The sounds of falling rain only tormented them. They could hear faint celebrations in the distance. They felt surrounded by the laughter of others.

Nathaniel stewed, feeling Kaiser was mocking him. But

before he could act, Savanna stopped him from going further. Instead, she guided his hand along the ground, writing *rebuild*. Guiding themselves along the way, they noticed different parts of the ground gave off different vibrations. Feeling their way up from underneath their feet, they touched what felt like a rock. Nathaniel noticed that it was a mountain. He gently held Savanna's hand. Despite not seeing each other, they were connected in a way. She knew that he had discovered a cave, even though it took her husband a while to realize that it was in a mountain.

Eventually the falling ash and rain stopped on both sides. Clearly, the song of silence brought anguish to everyone. They took no chances heading outside, but suddenly an intense burning sensation formed beneath their feet, turning unbearable. Panic ensued over what was going on. The mysteriousness led to confusion. What could be out there causing all of this? What had the power to burn the ground on which they stood?

Small fires started to engulf the inside of the shelters of the townspeople who had fled. Shell-shocked, they felt threatened, but nothing remarkable happened. All of them looked to each other in confusion. Everyone sought answers but remained afraid of the unknown, and they became hesitant to speak to one another.

Floria hugged her father. Kaiser had no choice but to lead.

"Who's out there? We are away from our shelters, is this what you wanted? Burning the very ground we stand on, and our shelters? Show yourself, whatever you are!" Kaiser bellowed.

The clouds parted. Heat from the sun's rays shone upon their faces. They felt its warmth. A small beam of blue light appeared in front of them, emanating from the sky, then it disappeared.

Edsel's breathing gained in frequency as he directed his fist towards Kaiser, the veins apparent on his face and muscles. Edsel shoved Kaiser to the ground, glaring at him, tearing at Kaiser's shirt with his right hand. "I don't know about you, Kaiser, but I'm leaving."

Lavinia ran towards her husband and demanded him to stop. But Edsel didn't listen. He thrust the index finger of his left hand on Kaiser's chest. "You know why I am leaving? I'm sick and tired of your demands. That goes for everyone in this town. My family and I have had enough of your demanding ways."

Edsel exaggerated, but no one else spoke up to defend Kaiser. Edsel spat on Kaiser's face, "Even your own flesh and blood is tired of your need to lead, even your beloved daughter. Can you believe it? Your own family is tired of being ruled. I don't know about anyone else here, but I'm leaving before the light comes back. Those who want to come, may. Those who don't, can stay here with whatever he is."

Edsel and his family, along with other townspeople, shuffled away. Floria was distraught to see her father helpless on the ground and she ran over to him.

The strange beams from the sky descended, drawing a line between Edsel and the townspeople, then disappeared. Over-confident, Edsel laughed, extending his arms. "We're free. See, I saved us all! Take that, Kaiser. I am the chosen savior."

Edsel grinned from ear to ear, staring directly at Kaiser. The beam of light returned. Everyone could feel its intensity. Heat radiated from the beam, herding them into a circle like animals on a farm. There was no avenue to run anywhere else; they were trapped. No matter how much they wanted to flee, they couldn't. Fires ignited, surrounding them.

A strong beam of light opened in the sky, piercing the clouds on both sides again. Something invisible descended. They couldn't see it, and the intense heat forced them to shield themselves. Their fears grew stronger when the sky went pitch dark, like it had done all those years ago. Memories came back to them. They were familiar with what was going on. They thought that it was the same event happening all over again and eased up a bit. Little did they know that it wasn't. The same loud rumble could be felt from underneath their feet, the same unknown warning sound could be heard blaring, the same red lights flashed in front of them. The townspeople knew to look up. They saw two bright, circular lights hovering over them. They were expecting whatever it was to leave, but instead the lights lingered much longer than expected. They gasped almost in unison when an unknown craft appeared before them. It looked like a huge, winged creature with wheels and a nose cone at the front. The heat of the unknown craft could be felt when it lowered onto the brittle dirt below.

Two strange, enormous beings emerged. Towering over the humans, they resembled Adina and her family. However, these beings were much larger and more intimidating. They had exposed wires and bolts lining up their huge robotic bodies, built with large wheels on their backs, but their faces looked human-like and their eyes were also human. At least Adina and her family only had exposed wires on their arms. Their ligaments and tendons were being held up by their metallic structure where the acid had eroded their bones.

The visitors stood firm, speaking to everyone with an authoritarian voice. "We're the Major Commanding Officials (MCOs) and High Commanding Officers (HCOs). We and everyone who lives here right now are on a planet named

Arawn. These lands are now known as forbidden land. It looks like our experiment worked well on the very land that everyone here stands on. Unfortunately, what you call home is no longer your home, but our home. Your planet threw us away so our planet lured everyone here. By creating a trap, we secured our boarders rapidly and created an invisible wall between each side, modifying the weather. We threw in implanted memories and created tension. Knowing your kind made it easier to ensure you blamed one another for the hardships. It's only natural for humans to do so. We control the very air you're struggling to breathe, but we wouldn't dare starve you of such a precious resource. All this time, we've allowed you to breathe and to survive this long."

"No, that's where you're wrong. We were here first, Annaecy is our homeland," screamed Edsel, clenching his fists.

"Did you hear me, human? You're in for a surprise, because that's where you're wrong. We kept everyone here alive for so long. We are no longer mere years into the future, more like centuries."

"What's that supposed to mean? I clearly remember that I've been here since I was a boy. Now that I ponder the suspicious series of events, Mortimort did vanish on that day when it became strangely cloudy. On top of that, it stopped raining when Adina left three months ago. She probably took the rain with her when her whole family became monsters." Edsel smirked. "But it was only a coincidence, if you ask me."

The military enforcements looked at each other. "You're such a fool to believe that it has only been three months and that Adina took the rain with her. The only thing that you failed to believe was Adina, and you should've listened to her. You still have no idea, but keep your limited beliefs."

Before the military enforcements could continue, Edsel rudely interrupted them. "Stop lying, we don't believe you. As far as we know, you're the ones that are invading our homes. And those are purely coincidences. No one has the power to control the weather, not even you."

"Foolish. I laugh at your misery, it's ignorance if you ask me. This planet was never your home to begin with. It's actually Century-70 and well into the distant future. We're artificially intelligent, our species has thrived here for long. We're far superior to humans. We built everything that you see here, provided to us by our own planet. Welcome to your new home of Arawn where you're going to be living from now on. Unlike you, we saw an opportunity and we took it even though we were broken and defeated. We repaired ourselves and made it our mission to set out on travels to explore this desolate land. We lured you to us and eventually we grew larger as a society."

Edsel laughed sarcastically at them and clapped his hands together when the strange beings finished talking. Kaiser glared at him and flapped his hand towards him to shush him, but Edsel didn't stop there. He folded his arms, rubbed his chin with his right hand and started humming loudly at them. The AI turned to stare at him to examine his rude behavior.

Kaiser grew furious with Edsel. "Let them speak, we've had enough of you running your mouth. After all, you were nothing more than an employee who worked for a corrupted mayor who thought he was above the law."

Floria ran over to her father and hugged him. Edsel smirked. "There you go, after all, your lovely daughter is protecting her beloved father from all the danger. Let me speak, Kaiser." Fumbling his thumbs, Edsel asked, "We could make a deal?"

"I am listening, human. What is it?"

"You allow us to stay in the town, and we won't do anything bad. We won't steal, we won't take your kind away and we won't hurt them. Take some or all of us if you wish."

"Your promises mean nothing to our kind. Humans do

nothing other than steal and lie to get what they want. We've no need for you. Our species doesn't use the restroom, sleep, eat or drink water. If you choose to join us, you must go to the other side and wait for the ashes to return, to become just like them. They're easier to manage. You may never leave here, you're forever imprisoned here. The weather is ours to control, sometimes it will rain or ashes will fall, or both."

"Don't leave us here, take us with you," Edsel pleaded, wanting to join them on whatever the strange craft was. He saw an opportunity and made a run for it. He met his fate as a bolt of lightning struck him, driving him to the ground and rendering him unconscious.

"Is there anyone else wanting to try?"

The question was met with silence. Everyone slowly backed away, afraid of what the military enforcements might do. Floria's eyes darted all around and she became nervous. She cleared her throat and raised her hand. The MCOs pointed at her. "Speak, human, what is it?"

Walking towards them, she said, "I would like to know what happened to my friend Adina, since you seem to have extensive knowledge of her whereabouts."

The military enforcements ignored her and walked away. They boarded their Arero Deluxe Transporter Aircraft and rose above, hovering over the humans below. An intense, high-powered beam lifted Edsel's unconscious body from the ground, passing it over to the other side. The MCOs considered the humans who lived on the other side as parasites and referred to them as louse. To the surprise of the MCOs, the louse raced toward the alluring heat and to the beam. Their plan was to block the paths with a circle of fire, but it didn't work.

"We could use this to our advantage to corral the former humans exactly where we want them."

Beams zapped the louse, leaving Edsel behind. The others

were elevated in a powerful beam of light before the aircraft disappeared into the clouds.

Rain poured on both sides of the town for a while, dousing the fires. It remained on one side when the ashes returned to the other.

All of the humans were considerably lucky. Every now and then, the AI species turned off the rain to let them grow crops. They lived inside caves. It was sad to hear Edsel's screams until the ashes silenced him. They couldn't do anything about it. After a while, the unknown aircraft returned to beam Edsel and took him back to Arawn.

It felt like an awfully long time, but the strange beings returned, bringing other strange visitors that looked like humans. But there was something about their eyes; they remained clueless. It was as if they were not completely there. They all had strange scars on their right arms like they had had something removed.

CHAPTER THREE
ARAWN

IT WAS NOW CR-90: During the last centuries, the landscape overall hadn't changed. A large dome covered the town of Arawn, nestled away from the forbidden land. Beside Arawn, on the further left side, rows upon rows of intricate structures lined the side of the military base and a tall water tower that only the Major Commanding Officials were allowed to enter. There was a form of secrecy among the officials. When there weren't any dust storms, the MCOs left the large dome open.

The military enforcements had some knowledge of the hidden wall and the mountains that had only appeared under their radar during the last few centuries. This was not widely known to the rest of the artificial intelligence species. The MCOs were unsure of what exactly was out there. To ensure complete power and control over their own species, the military enforcements created dust storms like they did on the forbidden land.

Large steal corridors connected to all the important pod shops within the center of Arawn. In the middle of the town was an alley where the louse lived. Pod homes dispersed from the alley so that the lucky ones lived far from it. Crimson and her mother lived near the alley, across from the Ganic and Asuma's shop. They were not the lucky ones. Since they lived near the alley, their pod homes were elevated higher than the rest. That way the louse wouldn't be able to climb their way to the top. The military enforcements often turned the AI into louse after they disobeyed their orders or betrayed them. They were stripped of their AIS•Cs and they had to wait until their bodies decreased in strength to a human level. Then they were sent to the other side of the forbidden land where it rained ashes so that they were turned into louse.

The younger, untrained AI were under the special guidance of the Major Commanding Officials. Their training begun when the first siren went off. After that, they were given three warnings, but really they were supposed to be outside the dome already by the first siren. If the second siren came on and a young AI missed it, they had to do whatever the military enforcements ordered them to do. They were ordered to understudy alongside the Ganic, they had to stand outside and be on guard at the military base, or help out at Asuma's shop which wasn't too bad, but Crimson wouldn't disobey the sirens. No one knew what happened if the third siren came on. She had only heard rumors about how the disobedient AI were sent to the forbidden lands.

The military enforcements were all divided into different tiers which were moderate, low, and highly skilled; High Commanding Officers (HCOs), Major Commanding Officials (MCOs), Low Commanding Officers (LCOs) and AI Soldier Species (AISS).

The highest skilled AIs were trained to live alongside the HCOs and MCOs in the military enforcement base. They always went where they were sent and did all the important secretive missions. The ones that were less skilled were assigned to join the LCOs. They were trained to look after the base, assist the AI medics in transporting AI species that needed to be repaired, and bring in the broken, younger AI. They also had to assist the AI researchers and haul debris into the factories to help them build more AI, but they weren't allowed to see the technology that was used. The less skilled AI had a greater advantage over the highly skilled ones; they were allowed to go home and see their families as they would rotate shifts. Most of the time they left their posts since nothing ever happened. The medic AI lived on base with the researchers along with the scientists and they didn't have any family. They were pre-programmed to keep on working.

There were a series of training tests that the untrained, younger AI had to undertake to determine who would join the highest-ranking tier. It all started with basic training, like running over medium-sized invisible barriers, walking a long distance, passing combat skill tests, and agility and strength training.

Crimson was under the guidance of the MCOs. She never liked going to training but had no other choice but to go. The reason she hated it was because she would always trip over or her foot would get stuck when she jumped, causing her to fall flat on her face. The young AI would laugh at her and make fun of her for not trying harder. They would mock her for failing all of her courses. She didn't have many friends as she preferred to keep to herself. She always passed the human studies, though, so no one wanted to be her friend, anyway.

Most of the AI weren't built the same. There were short, tall and medium ones. Crimson was a medium-sized AI, but even with her height advantage, she was the lowest of the low and didn't know who was who. It was a disadvantage even though she could easily scan and analyze anyone. She scored high on the human teachings for daily life, human emotions, and on everything from sounds to their histories. Of course, none of the HCOs would know if everything they taught her about humans was wrong. Meanwhile, her peers exceeded their expectations wonderfully. Even the small AI showed great strength and agility. Ever since Crimson had first been created in a factory all those centuries ago, she had known that she was different from all the other AI, but she wouldn't dare say anything or ask any questions. Despite failing the other portions of her training, her peers never shined well in their studies of humans and the HCOs seemed pleased. They were overall satisfied with their different rankings.

Other than learning about human teachings, the AI also learned about their own terminologies, even though they already knew what everything meant. There were a few teachers that thought it was not all that important to learn anything new, so they just told the students to repeat after them.

"An AIS•C stands for what? Artificial Intelligence Species Capsule. It's our lifeline, it keeps us moving and it often needs to be charged."

"What is the job of a VOXTER? The job of a VOXTER is to remind us of important pre-recorded details and to detect if we did our daily chores."

Something always happened when they were trying to learn the terminologies. The High Commanding Officers always got escorted by the MCOs to the secret water tower during training and the AISS didn't do anything besides stand there, which often led to the younger, untrained AI becoming curious. After all, there was always some form of secrecy among the superiors. No one was allowed to ask any questions unless they were deemed important. The younger AI who didn't pass their training were integrated back into society to see in which category the military enforcements put them in. If they had a special skill set, like mechanical skills, they were left to work with the AI researchers and scientists. If they showed any knowledge in medicine and tendency to help out their peers, they were left to work with the AI medics. The ones that showed little to no skills, like Crimson, were set to freely live out their life spans of twenty centuries. Their memories were then removed and they were destroyed and recycled to create more AI.

Right before the dust storms, everyone waited until last minute to pick up their charged AIS•Cs or to drop off the old ones to be recycled. Asuma was a jolly and happy hologram AI that appeared every time someone entered his shop. He looked like a hologram and not an AI, so most of the AI species forgot he was a hologram. He was built different, but the AI had no knowledge of how he had been created. Only the military enforcements knew. However, his shop was essential to the AI's livelihood. The front counter, the back rooms and the recycling room walls had massive, thin panels installed all around them. On the front counter were three containers, all labeled to make the process faster. Everyone dropped their AIS•Cs off in the correct container, and the machine then lowered them to their appointed destinations. It didn't take long, less than a millisecond. The AI formed a new line again if they dropped theirs off to be recharged or picked up. They stuck out their arm for their AIS•C to magnetically come back to them. If they were being recycled, then Asuma handed them over since he had to repair them when any mechanical issues arose or they had been broken. That was how Asuma kept track of everything, and he had a keen mind. He was also precise and intelligent but at times loved to talk too much.

The place was busy, and out of nowhere, Asuma laughed. "I hope everyone knows that the military enforcements are the ones controlling the dust storms on both sides of Arawn and on the forbidden land."

He committed a Freudian slip when talking. Everyone stopped talking when they heard what accidentally slipped out of his mouth. They assumed it was all true and believed that he did that on purpose, too. Even though the military enforcements caught wind of Asuma's slip, they never really did anything because he was the only one who had extensive knowledge of the AIS•Cs. On top of that, he built the intricate technology, deeming him untouchable by the MCOs.

Crimson headed home from training camp after not qualifying for the final rounds of training in front of the Major Commanding Officials. She knew her mother would be furious with her. She called Crimson wasteful at times. There was a lot of secrecy surrounding her mother as she refused to share many things with Crimson. She didn't know what her own mother did for work. Crimson didn't even know what her mother's name was, she always just told her to call her mother. Her mother had expressed not liking living next to the alley. Crimson was on high alert considering the alley was home to the louse. Their residence was pre-chosen by the MCOs, not by them. They knew about the danger of living next to the alley, but they refused to acknowledge the flaw in their design. Even though it was dangerous here, there was a small perk to living next to the alley. Directly across from where they lived was a long corridor, and that was where all the shops were located. Besides Asuma's shop, the second most essential shop was right next door. It was the Ganic maintenance shop, which was responsible for fixing all the intricate rows of technical hardwiring and reprogramming the IXS. The IXS-system controlled the closing of the pod home when it flipped over, and it was also the motherboard that controlled the pod homes. Only the Ganic maintenance services were equipped to handle the technical aspects of it.

Crimson unlocked the front door with her mind. The voice-activated VOXER greeted her, "Welcome home, Crimson. Your mother isn't home but she said to remind you to change your AIS•C."

Crimson ignored her mother's preprogrammed recorded requests. The VOXER recorded many of her movements before she even had a chance to tell her mother that she'd arrived. Her mother naturally extended her hand out in front of Crimson. A glowing blue light shined from her hand, forcing Crimson to freeze motionless. She was unable to move past her mother as her mother won every single time. Her mother went ahead and unfroze her, but as soon as Crimson began to speak again, her mother enclosed herself in a no-sound bubble, floating away and ignoring her.

Crimson and her mother lived in an interchangeable pod home inside a large dome that covered all of Arawn, minus the military enforcement camps, bases and structures. The large dome only opened when there weren't any dust storms. The pod homes had their own individual domes that covered them. The bottom of the pod home had an underground storage area that could be easily flipped over within their own pod home dome. A cushion helped with the decompression when the pod home flipped over, but they weren't upside down in any way. The downside was that it was not meant to be used as a living space. The IXS-system had to be working in a precise order and if they weren't careful when opening the dome, the louse could gain access into the home from the alleyway. The IXS-system also locked the loose items when the pod home was flipped over and was in charge of locking the underground storage containers for the safekeeping of the AIS•C.

The only access to the second level was down the stairs and towards the closet in the middle, away from the wall opposite the stairs. The sensors on Crimson's hand activated a large, circular knob which she turned counterclockwise to unlock an archway to a steel tunnel. A yellow safe light appeared at the top when it was safe to open the door. A key emerged and unlocked the back door systems, activating the flip of the pod home.

Crimson grabbed all the empty AIS•Cs at the bottom of the stairs, dragged out each of them and sorted them into the differently labeled bins at the storage center.

When Crimson was about to finish the last of the haul, the sky above became a complete void of darkness. A strange, blaring alarm could be heard in the distance. She wasn't quite able to explain its origin. The vibrations of a loud rumble could be felt and a surge of dotted white lights appeared all around. An overflow of blue search lights sought something, but nothing was apparent. Crimson couldn't explain what was going on.

Out of nowhere, a strange voice she had never heard before spoke to her from behind the storage center. "What are those lights in the sky? They must have known I was out here."

Crimson called out, "You think? Of course they already knew that you were here."

The unrecognizable voice spoke back at her, "Shh, keep your voice down and go hide, now."

Crimson dove behind the bins, spotting the intense light hovering over her, scanning and darting in different directions. Suddenly a massive explosion shook her. A plume of black smoke soon took over the sky and all the vivid lights disappeared along with the sounds. The darkness faded into the distance, leaving her to wonder what was going on. She looked around her, checking to see if she was hurt or if anything was damaged, and there it stood before her.

"Wait, please don't hurt me... I'm only fourteen years old."

An eerie quietness arose and a strange-looking species emerged. It didn't look like Crimson or any other kind of AI species, but there was something strangely familiar about it. It possessed the characteristics of a human, but there was no way a human could be standing in front of her. She looked closer at the specimen. It was wearing clothes. She was in disbelief, not actually comprehending what stood in front of her... a human, a real one, and the strange lights in the sky sought him. Crimson freaked out, not knowing what to do next. "No, you can't be. You're a human, but how? You can't stay here, what causes the lights to search for you?" She couldn't keep herself contained. "Wait, wait! No, no, no, this can't be happening to me. I am already a horrible young AI, I can't even pass a simple training test, and now this? Why me? Of all the AI, it had to be me. The one that fails every training."

"Umm, are you okay? Hello there." The strange human smiled nervously. "Wait, listen to me, could you just give me time to speak, please? I can explain everything. Hear me out, my name is Dexter and I come from Planet 6. It's my home, it has water, food, land and a lot of fun places to go. See, there was a strange occurrence and a vapor dust storm engulfed where I was standing. Didn't know such a phenomenon existed, but apparently it's common and random. That's how my uncle disappeared, my mother saw it all when she was a little girl and she told us all about it, unfortunately. No wonder my mom is overprotective of my sister and brother every time we go outside, now I understand why. There were water droplets, dust, and in the next moment, just like that, I'm sucked in! Rapid winds, like a vortex, whoosh, traveling at high speeds. This part is difficult to believe, but hear me out, it's exactly what happened to me. Everything around me turned black and the next moment, I'm screaming into blue skies. Since I saw blue skies, I assumed I must still be at home. It was all really just an accident, I was seriously thinking I was out of danger until I saw all the lights chasing me, and in no way did I actually believe wind was capable of lifting me up off my home planet and crash land me on this cushion thing here."

Crimson was confused. "What cushion?"

Dexter pointed to where he had seen it. "Come here, it's at the end of this."

Crimson was shocked. "That is not a cushion, it helps the house decompress when the house flips over and the Ganic has to look at the IXS-system. We'll have to fix it because your heavy mass broke it. Dust storms? Heavy winds? There are dust storms and winds here. How do I know you're telling the truth about how you got here? Planet 6?" Crimson was puzzled to hear of another planet. Rumbling sounded near her. Crimson caught her breath, on alert. "They're coming back, go hide."

Dexter was embarrassed. Looking at himself, he sniffled and fought his tears, blushing. "Well, actually... I have to go to the loo, that was my stomach. I hope you have crisps or chips? Where am I, by the way?"

Crimson wasn't sure what to do next. "Are you okay? Your voice changed. I recently learned about your kind. You're on Arawn, if you hadn't noticed. We don't look alike, minus our faces, my left side of my body and err... I guess our hair too? But mine is made up of wires and yours is made up of medulla, cortex, and cuticle. Anyway, we don't have chips or crisps, beds or toilets. My name is Crimson and I'm an Artificial Intelligence species, AI for short."

Even though Crimson had learned about the human emotions in camp, they never bothered showing how each emotion looked like. All Crimson could do was nod and try to understand the different emotions that Dexter expressed. She stood there staring at Dexter. "Wait? Aren't you from Earth? Didn't Earth get engulfed by fires due to the harsh climate?"

Dexter's tears fell from his eyes. "My voice changes when I'm crying. It's because you told me something mean, you called me fat and it's offensive to me because my heavy weight broke something." Dexter felt faint. "Wait! You're telling me I am not on Planet 6? No food? No loos? No entertainment? No nothing? Is there somewhere I could go... you know? Phew, I am feeling quite faint. We often get confused with Earth, but like you have already said, Earth burned away from the fires. Planet 6 was only created as a secondary planet with two seasons, winter for two weeks and a midsummer. My family and few other lucky families were brought onboard to travel to the new planet, since my mother and father are both researchers." Dexter still couldn't believe that he wasn't on his home planet. Even after Crimson had told him twice, he was still shocked.

Crimson spoke with confidence, "You're human, don't you have a heavy body mass? I am identifying your features as a human. I don't understand the complex human emotions. It looks like you're stuck here, Dexter. You landed on the wrong planet. If you want to eat something, all we have are rodents and the vermin from the forbidden zone... But we're not allowed to go there."

Dexter pleaded with her. "I am afraid of what they'll do to me. Can't I stay with you here? Please, let me stay here with you!"

Crimson folded her arms. "No way. Besides, I have to go back inside and get a specialist to repair the decompressor your heavy mass broke."

Dexter walked towards Crimson and threw himself on the ground, attempting to grab her by the leg.

"Watch it, I wouldn't do that if I were you. If I were to walk forward, I'd have flung you. Let go of me, now."

Crimson was attempting to deal with the unexpected visitor that happened to be a human. She tried to compute what would happen if the military enforcements found out what she was hiding. She headed into town, noticing the town was nearly half empty.

Asuma saw Crimson. "Crimson, hello? Is that you?"

Crimson greeted Asuma. "Yes, it's me, I got distracted by the few species walking around."

Asuma rumbled on. "I realize this sort of thing isn't uncommon. I have seen the lights and sounds as a young AI, too. But Crimson, don't tell the MCOs what I said. The whole town saw the lights and everything. Even the louse started to come out of the alley. The other AI species shooed them away."

Crimson interrupted Asuma, "Here are all the empty AIS•Cs."

"Perfect, I needed those. Wait, don't leave yet, Crimson. I have something here for your mother. I was wondering if you'd take it to her?"

Crimson couldn't shake the feeling created by the thought of what else could be beyond Arawn. Was there any way to return a human to its home planet? While browsing, she spotted a strange map tucked behind some books. Strangely, it didn't appear to be like the other maps on the stacks. It looked a bit old to be up for sale. Maybe Asuma had accidentally put it out. Almost malevolently, Crimson felt she might need this little map. Looking around her to ensure no one saw her, she quickly made the decision to tuck the map into the safe box in her chest. She shot a quick glance at Asuma. He had his back turned to her while grabbing things for her mother.

Asuma neatly packed the AIS•Cs and gave them to her. "Here you go, Crimson, these AIS•Cs should last at least three centuries. Keep bringing the empty ones back and we will have no backlog, guaranteeing no issues with the MCOs thinking I am not working effectively enough at times. I don't understand why they bother keeping me here all these centuries. Ignore me, Crimson, I always ramble."

Crimson often paid attention to Asuma, he was kinder than most of the adult AI.

When Crimson arrived home, the dome flipped. While she had been away, her mother had gone to see the Ganic. A million thoughts rushed through her head. What if her mother found Dexter? Or the specialist found him and went to tell mother? What if the MCOs already had him? Crimson saw the Ganic leaving and wasted no time in rushing inside, flipping the house. By the time she got there, it was apparently too late. Mother's arms were folded and she was standing by the storage shed. Dexter stood behind her, nervously laughing.

"You know what this is? This is a complete human, standing here. Do you know that these things eat? Sleep? Bathe? Use the bathroom? Do we have a bathroom? Food? Do you have any idea what happens to us if the MCOs find us in possession of a human? How does a human even get here? How did this happen? A human doesn't just land here out of nowhere. Explain yourself, Crimson. I'm waiting."

No matter how hard Crimson tried to point out the facts to her mother, it didn't matter. She refused to listen. Dexter intervened, trying to explain that Crimson was telling the truth. She had no choice but to accept his story, as unbelievable as it sounded. Mother gave Dexter some sort of special bars to eat. Crimson questioned why her mother had these special bars lying around and asked her directly why she had food for humans. Mother touched her own back. "I used to be human. I know that one day these will be essential, and it reminds me of my past."

Crimson was unsure how to react to learning her mother's secret. She pulled her mother aside and asked her if she would ever betray Crimson and turn Dexter in to the MCOs. She hesitated a bit. "No, I wouldn't, Crimson."

It left Crimson with even more questions.

After Dexter arrived, it got noisier in the house. A lot of talking and giggling went on as he and Mother would tell each other about life as a human. Crimson often wondered how she knew so much about human life. It piqued her curiosity.

Everyone was on standby, monitoring the cobalt blue skies above the domes. Warning sirens increased as a precaution. The MCOs ordered everyone into their pods to seek shelter from the dust storms. Within a second, the skies transformed into a menacing swirl, dusting the domes with orange dirt. Every time there was a dust storm, the louse roamed the street. No one really knew why they left the comfort of the alleyways.

Before Dexter entered their lives, there hadn't been anything fun for Crimson to do besides sit quietly in the safety of the pod home with her mother always ordering her around. Crimson wondered if her own mother hated her, or if her existence just irritated her. But who really knew? After all, she might not have liked her at all.

Crimson noticed Dexter sitting by himself. Carefully analyzing Dexter's expression, she couldn't tell what Dexter was feeling. This emotion was the one where she had stalled during the pop quiz. What was the emotion, though? Discomfort? Sadness or feeling uncomfortable. Not quite himself lately.

Crimson sat down next to him. "Dexter, are you okay?"

Dexter looked at her while playing with his shoelace. "Oh... Crimson, I didn't see you there."

Crimson nudged him on the arm. "Dexter, what's the matter? I'm sensing you have feelings, I believe you're sad... You have strange liquid seeping from your eyes, is that associated with crying?"

Dexter wiped his tears away. "I'm gutted, crying for sadness. It's been fun staying with you and your mom, but I miss my family – my mum, dad, sister and brother. I didn't get to see my father often, he unfortunately lost his mind, but I went to visit him every day at the hospital. A year later, he was starting to make a recovery. He did come back home after the nurses gave him the clear. Barmy, but I'll talk about it one day, not now. I miss my hometown of Newvert, I adore how it is surrounded by a forest. My favorite part of living there, though, is going to the cinema, to the playground, to the mall and, what I do mostly at home, is playing video games and going to the fridge to get food. There are random dust storms there, too."

While Dexter and Crimson talked about him missing home, the VOXER warning siren blared from different parts of the dome. "Dust storm arriving. Dust storm arriving, seek shelter now. Dome inversion imminent. Warning, dome inversion imminent."

Dexter expressed being afraid of the unknown dangers outside. He was familiar with dust storms as he had got sucked into a whirlwind before, but he thought he was going to be sucked out of this dome and land on another planet, somewhere worse. Crimson's mother ran over to him and tried to bring him comfort, but it didn't work as his worry was catching up to him.

CHAPTER FOUR
THE JOURNEY

"MOTHER, do you know how to get Dexter home?" Crimson asked.

"Yes, I do, but it's more complicated than just gathering a few ingredients here and there. There is a book I need, along with a little map. Rumors indicate the book is with the louse, but who knows? Last I heard, it happens to be heavily guarded by vicious creatures living in a cave. Unfortunately, that part of the cave is unknown or not explored enough to be mapped. Still, no one knows how the creatures came to be. Some say you need a code in their language just to open the doors to the vault. Anyone can go inside the cave, but it's dangerous because of the creatures."

Crimson then remembered the little map she had stolen from Asuma's shop. She didn't dare to take it out to show her mother because she knew her mother may have had an underlying objective to do something sinister. Just like when she had asked her mother if she would betray her by turning Dexter in to the military enforcements.

"Mother, how exactly do you know all this?" Crimson asked. Her mother was bothered.

"Crimson, shut your mouth. I didn't raise you to question. I'm an adult AI and you're just a young AI, you don't know anything. It's best to zip it."

Crimson pressed her for more information about the map. "Do you know anything about what this little map looks like?"

"Yes, actually, quite a bit. It has words on the sides. I also heard that if you put it before a mirror, you can read the words. They are backwards. There is a mirror in that drawer over there on your right, top drawer. A little boy named Finder taught me how the map works. They say if you get to see the map, the clue unlocks everything and anything your heart desires."

Crimson extended her arm, freezing her own mother. Startled, Dexter slowly backed away. Crimson moved Dexter out of the way, then encased her mother and stored her in an unknown part of the pod house. She pulled out the map and saw it was exactly as her mother had described. It was the solid clue to everything.

Dexter flinched a little. "Crimson, what was that? Did you just attack your own mother?"

"No, Dexter. I suggest you remain quiet. Even though she said she wouldn't turn you in, I still had my doubts. I know she was human once upon a time, but it doesn't explain how she knew a lot about how to return you back home."

She noticed the letters on the map were backwards. This was what her mother had spoken of. Dexter ran to get a mirror and grabbed food bars from the cabinet along with clothes and a bunch of other things. He held the mirror up to the map as Crimson held it.

Crimson spoke, "*He who holds the map will find his way home. Only friends from different worlds find their way with work. Two worlds meet at this time, causing each to separate, but each world will not become one. Warning: You are not allowed to take anything home from another's world. Friends need to descend into the cave and open the book but beware of the vicious species protecting the cave."*

"I'm buzzing, a real adventure," Dexter said excitedly. "I'll just put everything in this knapsack."

Crimson went to grab extra AIS•Cs before stepping out of the door. "Go right ahead, Dexter."

They made their way towards the alley without stirring any suspicion among the other AI. "Okay, let's go. Hurry, keep up with my pace, Dexter, or at least try to."

The louse smelled a human entering their alley and were soon on high alert.

"Oh no, it looks like the louse are attracted to you, Dexter, because you're a human. They must be picking up your scent. Stop, louse! Look, I made fire," Crimson threatened, moving her hands and producing a flame. The plan backfired. Instead of the louse being afraid of the fire, they quickly surrounded Crimson and Dexter.

"Look, Crimson, the fire isn't working. They aren't afraid of it. What are you going to do now?"

Crimson created a massive fireball and shot it down the alley. The louse pursued it. With the louse distracted, Crimson wasted no time grabbing Dexter's arm and guiding him down the alley.

Without a plan, Crimson didn't know what to expect once they had passed through the alley. She noticed that there was a light coming out of a crevice and spotted a large wall near them. The sun beamed on them. They were near where the wall wasn't protected by the dome. She helped Dexter climb over the wall. From atop it, they could see mountains on both the right and the left side of the town in an L-shaped formation. They made their way toward the right-side mountain range. Once they entered it, Dexter noticed one side of the mountain was dark with tiny specks of light shining through. He suspected they were stars but had no idea what it was for sure. "Wow, this reminds me of home," he said.

They walked further into the cave. Dexter was in awe, watching the night fall across the cave walls while the rest of the cave shined in daylight. Crevices, ridges and stone stairs were carved into the rocks of the mountain. Intricate arches filled the dark hallways hewn into the stone.

"Crimson, do you know the book? Your mother said there was a strange language in it. What lives here, should we be concerned?"

By that point, Crimson didn't know what to say because she didn't know the answers. Dexter's cheeks flushed. He started to sweat, announcing that he needed to use the bathroom.

"Like really, terribly bad. Where can I go?" Dexter begged. "I need to go, right now."

"We haven't traveled far, you want to go now? Go into that tiny cave in there. Cover it with sand when you're done, because if you don't, the strange creatures who live in the cave will pick up the scent and locate us."

Crimson gave him an extra push towards the tiny cave's entrance, ensuring no bathroom accidents happened. While Dexter went about his business, Crimson processed what her mother had said to her. Her mother knew everything about this cave and that book. What if she was one of the bad ones? The ones who passed over to the wall to explore this side? That would explain her suspicious behavior.

"I'm ready," Dexter announced.

"Did you cover your human waste with sand? We are unsure what exactly lives here and we have to be cautious with what we leave behind."

Dexter's cheeks flushed bright red. "Maybe I didn't?" He stopped, staring at her, then spun and ran back.

He returned a few minutes later. "There, I am finished."

Dexter played with his fingers. "It's amazing being on your planet and all, but nothing was like this on Planet 6. What is it like? You know, being your kind?" he inquired.

"You wouldn't want to be like us, Dexter," Crimson responded. "Our species are not allowed to think, we live differently. We are protected in this dome. What we are doing right now isn't allowed. Our life is predestined for our species. Let's keep going, Dexter, we'll talk more later. We must climb the mountain before whatever lives here finds us."

Crimson jumped and grabbed onto the higher ledge. She extended her arm over the ledge. Dexter kept turning his head to the right. Dexter stood on his tippy toes since he was still a six year old kid and short. He grabbed Crimson's hand and she pulled him up. That was when Dexter looked down, noticing a familiar sound. "Water? No way."

Dexter's eyes beamed with excitement once he saw the stream of water. "How come you didn't tell me you had water all this time? How I miss the sound of water, the thirst is getting to me. Smashing, I can fill up my canteen! Can I just fall in? It's safe, at least for me... I promise."

Crimson looked over. She was in disbelief. She had little to no knowledge of the existence of water on her planet, but again, she had never explored this side before. Dexter kept asking if he could jump into the water from where he stood, but Crimson was fearful because of how high up they were. She extended her arm over the ledge from where they stood to lower him down. Dexter carefully climbed down and jumped into the water.

"I wish that you could experience water. It's so cool, refreshing and wet. We use it to cook with, bathe in, sometimes it hurts, and it doesn't taste like anything. But it's healthy for us, at least that's what the adults and the doctors say." Dexter emerged from the water and shouted at Crimson if she could lower his backpack. He unzipped the backpack while still standing in the foot-deep water and pulled out his clean set of clothes.

Dexter kept turning his head to his right. "Umm Crimson, it looks like there was an underground cave down there in the water."

Crimson knew that she had to jump off the ledge, but the thought of getting into the water was another thing. Having no other choice, she jumped in. Nothing happened, so she walked into the cave and began to experiment some more with her AIS•C. She extended her right arm... turned her hand to make a fist down motion. Nothing happened. She aligned her right arm and left arm at the same time, simulated movement at the same time and swung her fists in a downward motion. An intricate, small beam of light appeared in front of her, forming a map of the mountains that expanded all around her. Walking deeper into the cave, the water wasn't stable and splashed on her. There wasn't anything to be worried about since the water didn't harm her in any way. Like she thought it would. Dexter was afraid of the darkness despite having Crimson's light shining on him. Her AIS•C light changed into three red dots that formed at the same time, indicating a presence of a target or an enemy near where Dexter stood. It dodged in and out of the darkness, undetected by Dexter. Crimson was immediately moved to high alert by whatever was lurking in the dark. She ignited a flash of light towards the shadows.

The light shot over a lone, scared creature. It was startled by the unknown being next to it as it jumped from its shelter in the rocks.

"Wait, don't hurt me! I speak! I mean no harm. I'm friendly. My name is Finder," the stranger announced and held out his arms, empty palms extended as a signal for peace. Crimson moved the bright light away. She couldn't believe what she was looking at. The resemblance was uncanny. "Finder looks like Dexter in that he, too, looks human, but he isn't."

Crimson didn't realize that she accidentally spoke that out loud. Both Dexter and Finder squinted their eyes, but Finder ignored her. "What are you? I've never seen your kind before. What are your names?" said Finder.

Dexter was too frightened to speak, so Crimson spoke for him. "This is Dexter, and my name is Crimson."

Dexter looked at Crimson, slightly confused, because Finder resembled him.

"According to your facial expressions, you must believe that I am a human like Dexter. My special skill is becoming a shadow, but I am not sure how or why. I know that I am different. I am an Entitylst Species, but before you freak out, I'm not the enemy," Finder continued after a brief pause.

"Is that why your name is Finder? Since you become a shadow and find things?" said Dexter.

Finder happily smiled at Dexter. "Yes, you're correct. On the upside, I found an old book in an old, smelly part of the cave and it has codes in it. I've lived here long enough to observe my surroundings, and being a shadow at times helps me become stealthy. There are two different species, the Entitylst and the Entitylst Soldiers. They speak Zectic and the soldiers possess long necks, fangs, rusted skin, they're hairy and vicious, and they need to be charged. The Entitylst are hairy, possessing red hoods. They also have long necks but don't require charging."

"You found the old book? Where?" begged Crimson. "Can you take us there?"

"Sure." Finder said, then noticed her arm. "What is the glowing thing you have on your arm? It's cool. Can I touch it?"

Crimson and Dexter both stepped back as Finder neared.

"You can't touch it," Crimson replied. "These glowing things are called AIS•Cs, they are my life and I depend on them. Dexter doesn't require one. He is a human, goes to the bathroom, sleeps and eats food often. Okay? Let's keep on going."

Finder noticed that Dexter was scared of the dark and he walked over towards him, extending his hand out. Dexter held Finder's hand and smiled.

"We can stop walking for now. We have walked approximately fifteen miles all totaled, climbed mountains, descended stairs, traversed long hallways and are now underground. That should put us somewhere in the middle of the Entitylst Soldiers. They're probably standing above us, don't make a sound. Their hairs are able to detect the sound waves and any vibrations in the ground," explained Finder.

"Is that what they tell you?" Dexter asked with a smile.

"It's often true, but don't worry. They won't notice we are down here," said Finder.

Dexter climbed on Crimson's back and she held him firmly, Crimson, Dexter and Finder sped away. darting to the left as Finder dodged to the right. Finder was insanely fast. Crimson was surprised he could keep up with her. She knew she couldn't run forever without checking on her AIS•C status, plus what made her afraid was her standing as a young AI. She wasn't fully aware of her powers within herself. In the distance, she saw high mountains reaching skyward. Crimson doubled her speed, but Finder couldn't keep up. Barely missing the tip of the mountain, she made it safely on a flat surface and Finder did as well. Dexter got off Crimson's back while she checked her AIS•C. They crossed an archway to get to the other side of the mountain.

CHAPTER FIVE
DECODE

CRIMSON, Finder and Dexter made their way towards the section where the Entitylst were on guard nearby. That was where they saw a huge, brown door covered with a bunch of weird indents possessing different depths and textures. Crimson wasn't sure what it meant. Finder observed Dexter, who was deeply concentrating on the door in front of him, snapping his fingers together, studying his surroundings. That's when it all came rushing back to him. "I know what these are, Crimson. These are numbers and each number is secretly a letter spelling out a word."

"You're right, Dexter. I've seen the long lost Zectic language but this isn't it. But how? Did it get lost in translation?" said Finder.

Crimson was not able to understand any of it. The MCOs hadn't taught her anything about translation in the camps.

Finder felt like they were fine on their own now and had everything they needed. "I feel like you don't need me to be here with you to assist you on your journey anymore. Until next time, if you need me."

Crimson and Dexter parted ways with Finder. Dexter

became somewhat overwhelmed because he wasn't sure if he really knew anything about the ciphers. He studied the door and Crimson observed him struggling a bit. The numbers were 15141225 18514 208919 151435 2392081521 20 2215935. But he didn't say anything; the door had a warning on it. All he could do was stare at Crimson to see if she noticed. She did, and his eyes darted away.

"What gives, Dexter?"

"Crimson, I need you to listen to me," Dexter urged. "This is not a joke. The door gave me a warning I can't read out loud. You need to stay quiet. Is there a way we could be connected? Figure it out, and hurry."

Crimson felt like something bad was going to happen if she didn't find a way to do so. Observing the guards, she saw they were at 89 percent, almost all charged up.

Dexter, I have an idea. I know that there is a way to become invisible, I've heard Asuma rambling on about it. Here, hold my hand. She immediately spoke under her voice,

"Come on, Crimson, you must focus. I must connect to the both of us... focus, connect, focus... deep breaths, come on, Crimson."

She looked at Dexter, telling him to focus and not to worry, she was going to connect to him but he had to remain calm. An intense breeze went underneath her and around Dexter. They both had big smiles on, it had worked.

A loud unlocking sound echoed through the cave. The Entitylst began to wake from their long charge. Racing to solve the puzzle before the Entitylst awoke, Dexter and Crimson looked to each other. Dexter held his breath. "It says, 'only read this once without voice.'"

All Crimson saw were numbers, entrusting her friend to decrypt the code. Then the cipher started to disappear slowly.

"Hey, look! There's another one," Dexter announced.

"Quiet, Dexter, no talking. Just use your inner voice or thoughts."

Dexter analyzed the door as the numeric code started to appear. 1516514 2085 82038 2015 2085 4151518 1144 2018116 2391212 1516514. Crimson noticed several of the numbers were the same as in the previous one.

"You see here, Crimson? Some of the numbers are the same, so they're the same letters."

"Yes, I am seeing the similarities between 1 – O and 14 – N, those seem familiar."

Dexter focused his gaze on the door. His eyes were concentrated as he read the cipher. Placing his hands on the door, he ran his fingers across the numeric code. OPEN THE HATCH TO THE DOOR AND THE TRAP WILL OPEN.

"What? No, no, this must be a trick. Did you do it wrong, Dexter?"

"No, it's what the code is. It's all correct. We need to trust this, it might be the only way to get through the door. Look, there are other numbers here that are backwards too, but you see, once we solve them, it will disappear as well. Then it will be followed by another set of numeric code."

They proceeded to the hatch, opening the door to the right. It clicked with every turn, but there was a problem; the door refused to open. Crimson and Dexter looked at each other, wondering if they had just activated a trap. The concern vanished the second they noticed the Entitylst had stopped in their tracks.

"What is going on? Crimson? Is this normal?"

The Entitylst were not moving. They began to think that opening the hatch had triggered something.

"Let's keep reading, Dexter. What is next?"

The solved numeric code disappeared slowly as another appeared. 225 2011191472081855 1920519 2131123118419

2085 2018116 2391212 19520... 10211920 231920. Dexter reviewed the puzzle but did not know how to solve it. There were too many numbers, making it all a blur. They all started to look the same. Crimson sensed his panic and placed her hand on his, looking at him and smiling. Dexter moved his hands to the door handle and exhaled, speaking with the voice in his head.

BY TAKING THREE STEPS BACKWARDS THE TRAP WILL SET... JUST WAIT.

He took three steps backwards. One... two... three... A loud clacking sound echoed through the cave as traps beneath the Entitylst began appearing. One by one, they were trapped in cages. Dexter looked at the door as the numeric code disappeared and another one appeared in its place. 19165111 152120 25152118 14113519. Dexter expelled a huge sigh of relief. SPEAK OUT YOUR NAMES.

"It wants us to speak our names, aren't they going to hear us?" Crimson asked.

"Crimson, let's just go with it," said Dexter.

"Crimson!"

"Dexter!"

The solved numeric code disappeared once again, this time faster, as another one appeared. Dexter focused his concentration on the door, this one was longer than all the others. 4531545 2085 1351919175 1144 2085 8944514 1451919175 2391212 116165118. DECODE THE MESSAGE AND THE HIDDEN MESSAGE WILL APPEAR.

6914497 2085 11525 135114 6914497 2085 1141923518. FINDING THE KEY MEANS FINDING THE ANSWER.

Dexter kneeled, touching all about the ground to search for the key. Crimson wondered, what key? It was like they had both hit a stump along the way. All the puzzle solving seemed as if it was a complete waste of time. A completely wasted journey.

They both heard the door clicking, noticing the hatch starting to turn to the left and leading them to think the door was relocking itself. Dexter held his breath, and it happened. The door opened. Dexter expelled a huge sigh of relief. "Let's go inside before it closes, unless you want to stay here? We'll see if the Entitylst start moving again."

Dexter and Crimson sprinted inside, the heavy door closing right behind them. The ceiling was high, like a domed cathedral. Majestic sunlight entered the room through stained glass windows set directly before them. The colorful prisms reflected the light within, conveying a feeling of warmth in the room. The ground beneath them was inscribed with a perfect circle. Both the ground and the walls surrounding them were inscribed in cipher.

Dexter noticed a huge stone in the center of the chamber. He walked closer to it and touched it, but nothing happened. Crimson walked over and touched it, too. Out came a magical book. Emblazoned on the book was a purple gem. She moved it slightly, not understanding what it was supposed to do. Dexter noticed that when she moved it, the purple gem reflected the sun so that a faint purple light beamed out of the gem.

"Look, Dexter, this book is written in the Zectic language."

"That's what it is?" Dexter remarked. All he saw was random gibberish he was unable to read, but he understood the drawings. He had no problem solving the cipher, but this seemed too much for his brain to unravel. "Wow, what are those? Are there really planets we don't know about?"

"There are other adventures waiting to be discovered, Dexter."

Crimson opened the book, noticing it was ripped. A page was missing. The tears along the page aligned with the map she had taken from Asuma's shop. She set the book down, carefully unrolled the map and placed it back in its place. A burn fused it back together, again becoming one page as it was meant to be. She pondered how Asuma had obtained the map. Unless he had known more about this place before? Then it hit her. It was Finder. He was the one who gave every single visitor important details.

Dexter blinked in amazement as an "X" appeared on the map. Shortly after, a path showed up, followed by codes and symbols. An arrow indicated to turn the page, fading once the page was turned.

Turning the page, the cave they stood in appeared. Soon a set of instructions revealed themselves, explaining how to open the portal. The bottom of the page provided more numeric code, but parts seemed to be missing... 239208 9 1919175.

When Crimson closed the book, she noticed the sunlight reflecting off the gem, once again producing an intense purple light. Dexter spoke up, telling her what he had seen when she had moved the cover the first time. Already standing in the middle, she aligned the gem, causing the purple beam to bounce off the cave walls and illuminate portions of the numeric code on the walls. 239208 208919 71211919 69144 2085 8944514 1351919175. Crimson saw some of the cipher code resembled that in the book.

Dexter spun around, ready to solve it. "239208 208919 71211919 69144 2085 8944514 1351919175," he spoke. "With this glass find the hidden message."

The purple light soon dissipated back into the gem and the heavy book threw itself to the ground. A light filled the whole room, giving off an even brighter illumination than they'd grown accustomed to. Shielding her eyes, Crimson saw a stone book transform itself into a real book, the pages rapidly turning by themselves. The bright light dissipated as it stopped at a blank page.

Curiosity took hold of Dexter, who instantly kneeled down to touch the blank page. The code revealed, WITH THIS GLASS FIND THE HIDDEN MESSAGE.

Dexter stood next to Crimson, flipping through the blank book. He scratched his head, confused. Nothing seemed out of the ordinary. Dexter repeated, "With this glass find the hidden message."

It dawned on him that there had to be a magnifying glass of some sort somewhere in these pages. Dexter smiled at Crimson. Then he turned to the back of the book, touched his hand on the page, and found the magnifying glass. "This is it, I found it. This is called a magnifying glass, it will show us something hidden."

"Dexter, with this glass, we can see what this page is telling us. It's a set of instructions to open the portal," Crimson said. She used the magnifying glass, hovering over the pages as she turned them. About to give up, she opened a page and noticed a faint, sparkling light coming from the middle of a gem drawn on the page. Once again, carefully guiding the sunlight into the depiction of the gem, she made an intense light hit the magnifying glass. Millions of intricate lines reflected off the cave walls. Crimson could not maintain her hold of the magnifying glass as the brightness of the light began to turn it glowing red in her hand.

Dexter could smell something akin to metal being burned. The brightness consumed the cave, then the rays started burning holes in the book. He was blinded and threw himself to the ground, shielding his eyes from the light.

Crimson let go of the magnifying glass, causing the light to disappear, but the damage was already done. The heat caused large parts of the ground to disintegrate all around them. They were suddenly surrounded by darkness. The book was unharmed because it was a magical book encased with a special protection spell. Crimson turned over, looking at Dexter. She realized he was still knocked out from the heat and the intense light. Cautiously, Dexter opened his eyes, surprised he was still able to see. He rose slowly, feeling dizzy, and fell over. He fainted.

Echoes from behind the doors could be heard, as if the Entitylst were unlocking the system. Soon enough, they'd be able to spot Crimson and Dexter. In the midst of the chaos, the two became disconnected from each other. The ground beneath them started to crack into pieces. It wasn't long before the Entitylst found them.

Crimson quickly came to her senses and moved towards Dexter. They had to get out of there before the ground beneath them completely fell apart. Unsure what to do when the Entitylst ran towards them, Crimson wanted Dexter to get up, but it wasn't possible. The cave walls around Dexter had already disintegrated and the ground shook forcibly. Crimson held the book close to herself, making her way to him. A large piece eventually broke off, falling into an endless darkness. Above her, she observed the Entitylst pointing towards them and calling inaudibly, floating away. They had arrived too late to destroy them. The rest of the room fell apart around them, eventually crumbling into the darkness. Drifting away, they saw a huge, fiery mass bounded in complete darkness.

Dexter woke up. "Hey, look, we're in space. Is that small planet in the distance your home?"

Soon enough, the planets aligned as shown on the map. Arawn, Renu Claw and Planet 6. Realizing there were more planets, Crimson looked to Dexter, confirming neither knew anything else existed outside of Arawn and Planet 6. The military enforcements had never taught this.

"Look at the big blue planet with the large, metallic structure, Crimson. It's my home, Planet 6."

A light appeared from the book, contacting the unknown planet and rapidly drawing them into the unknown. Not knowing what was next on their journey, they descended into a distant planet's hemisphere, mysterious forces breaking their fall.

They were surrounded by fluffy clouds, a lake, and trees only recognized by Dexter.

CHAPTER SIX
FOREGONE OF ALARIC

IN A STEEP, verdant meadow, a frail old man ran with adrenaline rushing through his veins. His body felt as if he were a young lad once again, rushing down the mountain. His feet ached with every stride and from scraping the sharp edges beneath his toes and heels. The momentum caused his chest to pulse sharply with every beat by the time he reached the bottom of the ridge. With his last breath, he propelled himself towards the guards in an attempt to get past them. Sadly, it wasn't enough. They simply grabbed him by the arms before he could enter the castle.

"Halt! What brings you here? State your name, peasant."

"They call me Strange Old Man. Please, I beg, let me pass. I have an important message for King Dimitri. It's urgent," the breathless old man pleaded.

Dimitri heard the disturbance outside and strode towards the man. "Stop! What brings you to my castle?"

Strange Old Man fumbled with his words. "I... I..."

"Speak up, fool," King Dimitri urged.

"I'm afraid you won't believe me. I know what happened to

your wife," the old man said, squirming against the guards' tight grip.

"Guards, let him go. What do you know?" asked the king.

Gulping and frightened, Strange Old Man replied, "A powerful witch lord by the name of Hayden Harper has her. Everyone in the land fears him."

"Sir? Sir? What should we do with this man? Are you going to believe him?"

"Yes. Let him in," Dimitri replied.

The guards pushed the peasant through the castle's gates.

"My king, if I may speak? I urge you, Hayden Harper is a powerful witch lord, capable of doing anything he pleases. He can do the worst to people, cast dark spells on anyone trespassing against him."

Dimitri spun around. "Wait, Strange Old Man, I caused no harm to this witch lord. I don't even know what he looks like. He sounds like a scared, weak-minded fool."

"You don't need to know him or trespass against him. Since you're the king, he is planning on casting powerful spells on your wife."

Dimitri clenched his fist, his temperature rising. His nose flared with every breath he took. "That's enough," he yelled. "I've had enough of your lies. You're going to tell me, this instant, where Hayden Harper lives at this moment."

Sensing the king was distressed about what had happened to his wife, Strange Old Man tensed. "I only know what I heard, no one else dares to come forward with the rumors they hear in the town square, only I was brave enough to face you, sir." Strange Old Man's teeth clenched as he started feeling faint. "I don't know where he is at. At this moment he... doesn't exist."

Dimitri grabbed the peasant by his tattered shirt collar and shook him. "What do you mean, he doesn't exist?"

"Sir, I know you don't like being lied to. Please, I beg you,

King, don't hurt me. My wife is expecting a daughter," Strange Old Man whimpered and sobbed before the king as he threw himself to the ground.

"You know what, I'll make you a deal. I'll spare your life if you show me where Hayden Harper lives. Now, do we have a deal?"

Strange Old Man made the deal with the king without reflecting on the consequences.

Strange Old Man was convinced Hayden Harper was at a cabin. From what he had heard in the town square, Hayden Harper dwelled in the darkened forest.

The guardsmen prepared hunting tools and folded them in blankets, tucked safely inside their satchels, and helped the peasant onto a horse. Reaching the darkened forest, the horses became paralyzed with fear, neighing and refusing to go any further.

"Sir, it is best we stop here to rest, the horses are startled by some unseen danger ahead. We are not certain of these woods at night. We have cleared an area to camp here tonight. We can keep the prisoner bound to a tree to make sure he does not run away."

Early the next morning, the sun should have risen, but it didn't.

"Why is it still dark?" the men wondered.

Strange Old Man explained, "This is the darkened forest, where the sun doesn't shine. It's where Hayden Harper lives, a man of mystery and one whom you shall never want to encounter. People use his services to obtain something or to seek revenge. He collects souls, casting them into the dark underground. Those who seek him wish they never did."

They walked a mile further into the darkened forest. Sure enough, Hayden Harper's abandoned cabin was spotted. It showed signs of decay. An overwhelming sense of despair overwhelmed the guardsmen as they entered the cabin. It was dark, damp, and showed little to no signs of anyone ever occupying it, yet it was well organized.

"Sir, all we found was a letter on the desk, signed by Hayden Harper himself. It reads: *"Sorry I have missed you! You found my cabin but not me, surprise! Did you really think I was going to actually be here? I heard you were coming, you'll never find us. That's right, Dimitri, she's beautiful, isn't she? There was no way you could hurt this kind face, how could she ever love a monster like you? Oh, by the way, she's expecting a beautiful daughter. Not that it matters, anyway. You'll never see her again. - Hayden Harper."*

Dimitri clenched his fists, enraged, and grabbed Strange Old Man violently by his collar, thrusting him onto the ground. The guardsmen restrained the king.

"Look, you fragile old man, I don't know what sort of sick game you're playing. My best bet is you're working with the witch lord Hayden Harper himself. You're one of his souls, he's controlling everything you do for him. Do I have it correct?"

The old man pleaded with the king, "No, my king, you have it all wrong. I am not working with Hayden Harper, he hasn't taken my soul, yet. All he did was write a letter, somehow he knew you were looking for him."

"I don't know whether or not you're telling me the truth, but you didn't keep your word on delivering the witch lord to me. I'm not buying what you're selling me. For being wrong, you'll deliver me your unborn daughter as a consequence for your actions. If you don't, I'll take your wife and have her locked up."

"You want the truth? I'll tell you the truth. I knew nothing of Hayden Harper's whereabouts even though I said so, trusting on the possibility of finding him. All I wanted to do was to tell you what I heard. It was a rumor in the town square, everyone in town is afraid to face you. You cannot steal my daughter from me or lock up my wife, you have no right to do so."

The king clicked his tongue. "Well, that's where you're wrong. I am the king! I can and will do as I please. Especially after this little stunt you pulled, do you really believe you're free? You're simply a peasant, a nobody. I'll tell you what, I'll add a lump sum of wealth. Did it occur to you to think how you are ever going to take care of a baby? They eat, bathe and their schooling isn't affordable. Tell me, peasant, where are you going to get that kind of wealth from?"

Strange Old Man knew he couldn't take care of a baby. Tensing instantly, he bowed down and began kissing the king's feet. The king wasn't pleased with having his feet kissed, so his guardsmen threw the peasant into the woods.

Nine months later, Strange Old Man ran out of the Village of Alaric to give his daughter to the king.

"I have my daughter, sire! My beloved wife does not know she is missing. Please, I just ask of you, take good care of her."

King Dimitri fell immediately in love with her after holding her in his arms. Her eyes winkled with a magical spark. There was something in those eyes when she looked at him that reminded him of the sunset. He felt a warm love within her fiery, orange pupils. Every time she looked up at him, her smile was radiant. At her young age, she possessed a confident smile and the king saw her as his own.

Strange Old Man had no choice in giving up his daughter to the king for the lump sum of wealth. He even obtained a horse, a cow and a few pigs. It would be enough to sell, eat and to survive. Knowing he hadn't been able to lead the king to

Hayden Harper, there wasn't anything he could do, save give a last goodbye to his daughter.

Heartbroken and on his way home from dropping his daughter at the castle, the frail old man encountered Hayden Harper. He had not seen him before in person, he'd only heard of him through rumors and folklore in the village. Hayden was tall with scaly tan skin. Crow's feet etched his face that was surrounded by long and curly brown hair. He had two good front teeth, and his clothing possessed an antique feel. Colorful plaid pants fit snuggly on his waist and his voice was irritating as he spoke in a whiny, high pitched, piercing tone.

"Great performance back there," Hayden said, clapping at Strange Old Man. "Not only did you manage to bring down his entire kingdom but also the king himself. What I am most proud of is you attempting to lead him to me without confirming where I lived. Tsk, tsk. But look at you now, you've outdone yourself. Unfortunately, your soul now belongs to me."

Hayden Harper grabbed Strange Old Man from where he was standing and tore his soul away. Strange Old Man abruptly grew weak and fainted in front of Hayden.

Hayden had what he wanted and vanished, leaving Strange Old Man helpless on the ground.

The king didn't want to acknowledge his beloved Kingdom of Alaric was falling apart after he had spent all of the kingdom's money on finding Hayden. He had to stop at nothing to get revenge on him, but he was ashamed his kingdom no longer existed. It had been his decision to spend the money to actively search for Hayden Harper. The king spared nothing in an attempt to find his beloved wife.

Most of the people in the kingdom had already left, but his loyal armed guardsmen chose to remain by his side, sacrificing their families to stay. None of it mattered. The king grinned from ear to ear. "At least I have my daughter, Eden Alaric, now. I can start over again. My beloved wife would be so proud of me. She wouldn't approve of how I obtained the little one, but come on, there isn't much not to love about her."

The king wiped away tears, remembering the last day he had spent with his queen before she had disappeared. Dimitri took some belongings that reminded him of his beloved to his secluded log cabin, away from everyone in the kingdom.

No one knew what had happened to Strange Old Man after his wife found out about the disappearance of their daughter.

Years later, the Village of Alaric stood in ruins. It no longer belonged to Dimitri Alaric. The people remaining decided it was time to change the name to something that didn't remind them of their disgraced former king. The name Renu Claw was selected by those who had decided to rebuild. The villagers decided they needed to select a few trustworthy people to run Renu Claw because the last thing they wanted was to select another monarch to rule their village and run it into the ground.

Sadie went to Strange Old Woman's house to check on her wellbeing. Everyone in the village pitched in to help since she was an elderly woman. It was now Sadie's turn to receive the same help from everyone else in the village since she had given birth to a healthy boy, Zephyr. He was a handful.

Watching Sadie play with her son made Strange Old Woman jealous. Looking after Zephyr every day, the complete desperation got to her. Every night she looked to the moon for answers, hoping one day she'd be reunited with her daughter.

She was no longer able to mask her frustration over not being able to see her own daughter. She had pushed the anger down for so long.

The next morning arrived early, the sun peeking through the clouds and Zephyr looking up at his mother with his bright, light blue eyes. They resembled the ocean.

Sadie noticed the Strange Old Woman waking up. "Good morning, Strange Old Woman. I should be leaving soon, but I was waiting for you to wake up," Sadie said, smiling. "But thank you for looking after Zephyr. Let me go drop him off at Nedina's house and I'll be right back."

Strange Old Woman shrugged her shoulders and went about her day, returning to her home. She heard a frantic knock at the door. Thinking the worst, that maybe something had happened to Sadie, she rushed to open the door. Instead, it was one of the villagers acting strange. The villager struggled to speak.

"Sorry to bother you, but I bring an urgent message," the distraught villager said. "It's a message from the witch lord Hayden Harper. You must avenge your husband and now is your time to do so."

Strange Old Woman was confused. "What are you talking about?"

"It's true, he came to visit me in a dream. I was sent to tell you, and now I'm leaving town."

The paranoid villager ran into the forest, leaving Strange Old Woman baffled. She pondered the message she had received, softly closing the door behind her. All she could do was stand in confusion.

Strange Old Woman secretly hated her friend Sadie. She wished her daughter was with her. She eventually stepped out of her home. Descending deeper into the forest, not realizing how far she walked, she somehow found herself in the dreaded darkened forest. Complete desperation set in. Her mind was preoccupied by how her life could've been if her daughter was here with her.

A subdued voice coming from the forest spooked her. "If you want to find a way out, follow the dark sky."

Looking up, she stumbled toward the voice and found an abandoned cabin. Dropping to her knees on the grass, she sobbed, begging for Hayden Harper to return her daughter to her. "Oh please, please, Hayden, I beg you, bring me my daughter. I know that my coward husband gave her away to the king. In exchange, I will trade you my friend Sadie's beautiful young son, Zephyr. Come for his soul."

A strong gust of wind blew the cabin door wide open, sending her tumbling backwards. She couldn't believe who was standing in front of her.

Hayden Harper.

"Well, hello. That sounds like a fantastic idea. But I'll tell you what. I'll bring you your long-lost daughter if you can do one more thing for me. Give me your husband."

Strange Old Woman rolled her eyes at Hayden. "You can have him, he ruined my life. What does that have to do with my daughter?"

Hayden Harper produced a whirlwind, disappearing into it in front of her. It was the last thing she remembered from that day.

She opened her eyes outside the front step of her house. Embarrassed, she hoped no one had seen her. She raced inside, becoming paranoid and peeking back through the door to see if anyone noticed.

One of the villagers let out a scream of terror. It summoned everyone in the village from their homes. They couldn't believe what they were seeing.

"Hurry, I urge you. I've seen it move! There is something in the brush. I just saw a big toe, and it moved."

Sadie went to inspect this strange toe. All she did was poke it, and she heard a wail of pain come out from of the bushes. Everyone, including the children, were afraid.

An unknown male voice bellowed, "That hurts, who did that?"

Two arms broke out through the brush. Everyone gasped.

"Could it be true, the legendary tale of the long-lost man who went mad trying to find his way out of the darkened forest?"

What if it was real?

Everyone rushed to the brush, pushing the foliage down, only to realize it was a fragile old man. Sadie and other villagers ran in to help the frail man to his feet. Everyone in the village attempted to assist, cleaning the debris off the old man.

The villagers helped the old man to the home of a villager to clean him up. They groomed him, gave him a good shave, cleaned his unkempt toenails and fingernails, and applied cold water compresses to his aching teeth. Once cleaned and cared for, his identity was revealed. It was Strange Old Man. When he stood up, the villagers gasped. When everyone recognized the old man, they began to mumble under their breaths. "It's that bozo who gave his baby away to the king, let's not bother with this vagrant," he heard more than once. The crowd quickly dispersed. Sadie couldn't believe what she heard and rushed over to hug her dear old friend.

CHAPTER SEVEN
RENU CLAW (PRESENT)

CRIMSON HEARD a sound in the distance. They ran to the bushes.

The sound of fast hoofs scared Eden. "Zephyr, slow down this instant or I am leaving you! Can't you see the horse is frightened, and you're scaring me."

Eden hit Zephyr's back, wanting to be let off. He tugged on the reins, slowing the horse. "Sorry, okay! Okay, I'll slow down."

After reining their mount to a stop, Zephyr helped Eden off the horse, but she was already angered by her beloved.

The two people had dismounted before Crimson could say anything. Dexter covered his mouth, shaking his head.

"Even though you're angry at me, this is a nice spot to rest for a while, my love." Zephyr took her hand despite her being angry at him, gently caressing her cheek. "I am mesmerized by your eyes because your sun is my ocean."

Her fury melted. His caring nature was what she loved most about him. They both smiled at each other and held hands.

"What would our lives be like if we were to be married, Zephyr?" she asked, staring deep into his eyes.

"That day will be the most magical moment of our lives. I'll get to cherish every second with you, embrace you with all my love and shower you with blossoms from the sky."

Dexter broke the silence, laughing out loud. Love was mushy to him. All Crimson could really do was stand there looking at him.

Zephyr paused, cocking his head to listen. "Eden, do you hear that?"

Eden put her hand up to his chest. "Yes, Zephyr. Maybe it's just some kids from the village causing trouble."

"Eden, you know kids talk. They are going to tell the whole village about our forbidden love."

Zephyr carefully walked to the laughing brush, grabbing his sword. "You have until three to get out of the bush or I'll cut you down."

Before he could even commence the countdown, they walked forward.

"Please, don't hurt us. My name is Dexter, I am human like you. Can you tell us where we're at?" Dexter panicked, smiled nervously and Zephyr put his sword slowly back in its sheath. He smiled nervously at the two love birds standing before them. Zephyr put his sword slowly back in its sheath.

"Hi, I'm Crimson. I am not a human but an AI, but nice to meet you." She waved at them.

"Wait, you weren't really going to use that on us?" Dexter spoke nervously.

"Nope. I am not that crazy. My sword is only used for protection and hunting." Zephyr touched the hilt of his sword. Dexter became confused as to where they had landed.

"Could you tell us where we are? We landed on this planet.

Wait, did you say you hunt? I am hungry for real food, these bars aren't really food."

Eden ran to Zephyr, staring at both Crimson and Dexter. "Why, hello there! Welcome to Renu Claw. Did you say your names were Dexter and Crimson? And one of you is human? And the other isn't?" Eden was clearly confused as to what was going on. Crimson was shocked by her response; she wasn't afraid or even surprised.

"You're not curious to know where we arrived from? Or why I look different from the both of you?"

"No, I am not a judgmental person. I take care of children, the elderly and the sick, and I am not one to judge people based on their looks," Eden spoke kindly.

Crimson became confused. "We were lead here for some strange reason and I don't know why."

Zephyr turned to look at Eden. He thought that maybe they had bumped their heads along the way, and perhaps they were lost on their journey and confused. Zephyr looked up at the sky and saw that the sun was about to set. Night would be arriving soon. "Let's go, Dexter. We only have a few more hours of sunlight if we want to catch something."

Dexter turned his nose and was surprised. "Wait? Just hold on. So, you mean to tell me we catch something? Like an animal? You and me, to eat?"

Zephyr didn't know what was going on. He wanted to know if Dexter was being serious. "Yes, it's what we do in our village. We go out, hunt an animal, skin it, cook it and then eat it. I don't see another way."

Dexter didn't like the thought. He never went out hunting an animal, not by himself nor with others. Zephyr somewhat understood as to why Dexter wasn't eager to join him on his hunt.

Meanwhile, Crimson, Dexter and Eden set up a fire near a pond.

Eden became nervous when she looked at Crimson. "I have questions. Like, who are you? Where are you from? If Dexter is a human, how is it you're not? Why aren't you like the rest of us and what is the thing on your arm? Sorry for asking you so many questions, but I am curious."

Crimson tried her best to explain. "Well, for starters, I am not fully human but an Algorithm Intelligence Species. I have robotic parts, wires and bolts. You can see that I look like a human but I am really not one. Well, like you, sort of, kind of. I don't know how it works, but here I am. I live in a town called Arawn, in a safe zone, with my mother. Those not living in the safe zone are called louse. They live in an alley. Explaining why they're only allowed to live there is difficult. The MCOs are the ones keeping our kind safe, and the Entitylst live behind the wall, but we don't know much about them. We're not allowed to venture beyond the wall. I didn't know Dexter before he crash landed in my backyard. What makes me different from you and Dexter is that I possess AI technology, meaning I'm bionic and highly intelligent. What sets us apart from each other is we don't have emotions or perform any tasks humans do.

"The device on my arm is called AIS•C. Not to worry, we recharge three times before we return them to a special place. They're sorted and those that don't work are recycled to be used again to make new ones. I have special hardware that lets me see through things. I still don't know much, I am not an older Algorithm Species, I am just a young AI. I still have a lot to learn."

Eden didn't know how to make sense of everything. "Wow, knowing someone is here from the future makes me wonder what else is out there."

• • •

Zephyr didn't have a problem with Dexter hunting with him but he preferred to hunt alone. If Dexter was here, he would be asking random questions, that would become too distracting for him to hunt.

Since Dexter didn't want to tag along with Zephyr, Dexter went to the pond away from Crimson and Eden to give them their space to talk if they wanted to. Once he was finished washing up, he decided to take a nap and drifted off to sleep.

Unfortunately, Dexter was abruptly awakened by a nudge and pain coming from his foot. It was Zephyr nudging him awake. Dexter saw a rabbit in his hand and wanted to know how he had caught that. "Did you happen to catch that rabbit with a rifle?"

Zephyr stopped in his tracks, looking at Dexter, speechless. "A what?"

Dexter moved his hands. "A rifle. You do know what that is? It's a tool to hunt animals."

Zephyr rolled his eyes at him. "We don't have those here, I don't know what that is. Are you sure your head wasn't broken from the fall, Dexter?"

Zephyr also pulled out frogs and bugs from his tan satchel.

When Dexter saw that he instantly gagged. "Gross, frogs and bugs. Don't you have a fridge? Or a food container? A stove?"

Zephyr became angry with Dexter. "Why do you keep telling me weird and strange things, I don't know what they are. And weird wording?"

Dexter put two and two together. Did Zephyr really not know everything he was saying was true? Maybe it didn't even exist on this planet? He didn't want to think about it too much and started to feel woozy.

"Say, how are we going to cook this?" said Dexter.

Zephyr had enough of hearing Dexter speak. "A fire, what else? We don't have anything besides a fire pit, we put sticks inside of it and light a fire. Fire ovens only exist in the villages that have more currency."

Dexter started putting all the clues together he'd gleaned from Zephyr. It could only mean one thing; he was in a different era. People hunted for food the old-fashioned way without modern ovens, refrigerators and microwaves. So it meant he was in the past, which frightened him. He wasn't born yet and had no idea how to do things. He was confused. Zephyr found large leaves for Dexter to sit on, making him comfortable.

Despite Zephyr being annoyed with Dexter, he still had a soft spot for him and Crimson. Even though it was risky having these visitors in their home, he liked the change despite it being temporary.

"Have a seat, I made you a nice bed to sit on. I am going to start cooking the frogs and the rabbit."

Dexter held his nose and gagged some more. Zephyr laughed mockingly at Dexter, but he remembered the first time when his mother had given him a frog to try. He, too, had turned his nose and gagged.

Zephyr handed Dexter a leaf with berries, rabbit meat and bugs on it.

"Gross, bugs!" said Dexter.

Zephyr laughed. "Eat the bugs, they're good for you. It will give you energy for our journey back to my village."

Dexter picked up a large, fat worm.

"Wait, what are you doing, Dexter? No, no. You're doing it wrong. No one likes the taste of straight up bug guts. The way I gave it to you is the way you're supposed to eat it. Now, put it the way it was," urged Zephyr.

Dexter put everything back the way Zephyr had given it to him. He covered his nose and his eyes, then put the leaf, worms, berries and rabbit meat all in his mouth and started chewing, fast and loudly. Eden handed him a wooden cup with water in it. Zephyr laughed softly at Dexter.

Eden stood up and excused herself. "Nice meeting everyone, but I must get back to my father."

Zephyr stood up too. "Yes, my love, be careful getting back home. Don't worry about our new friends. I'll give them a place to stay."

Zephyr and Eden exchanged a kiss goodbye and he helped Eden back onto her horse. He watched her ride off. Then he put out the fire, gathered his supplies and packed for their journey. They all traveled to where Zephyr lived. It wasn't far. They walked away from the pond, straight through the marked path, and through the forest until they saw a large mound of trees and branches. Zephyr wanted to take a detour instead and show them the old castle to let them see the market. Dexter looked ahead and spotted a huge limestone castle. He was amazed, having never seen a castle in real life, only on television.

Zephyr grabbed the red picnic blanket and covered Crimson. He didn't quite understand her. In a way, she did look a lot like him. She had some skin on her face and on the left side of her, but she wore a metal plate on the front, covering most of her. "I'm putting this around you to keep people from asking too many questions. Welcome to the old castle. This area is for anyone who wants to head to the market to trade animals, cooked food, bread artistry, items for farms and all kinds of drinks. Then we usually head into the old castle. All of the castle rooms are locked, but not the center, and there are guards keeping watch on every hallway leading to a room door."

Dexter was overwhelmed by the sights and smells and all of the dancing. The smiling faces reminded him of home, and he found himself missing home even more. Zephyr pushed Dexter along as he thought that he was getting distracted by all the smells. "Come along, Dexter, we can't stay here all evening long."

They walked a short distance away from the castle.

"Well, we are here. This is where I live, welcome."

The overlapping canopy of million-year-old trees arched over the village. The sight was wonderful; the rigid detail of the trees, the evening sunlight showing through the openings between the branches. The trees had endured for so many years.

They walked through a long, intricate passageway in the darkness. It was filled with rows of concrete archways, entrances on both sides. The more they walked they noticed lanterns already lit. The floor comprised of dark blue, white, and tan mosaic tiles. The stairs leading down to the center of the town were made of concrete. Each of the archways led into a thoroughfare with homes and open land.

The town center was filled with vendors selling all kinds of household items, like carpets, furniture and jewelry. Sometimes the guards let them celebrate and usually the people would dance and sing. It got irritating especially at night since everyone was trying to sleep. It got irritating especially at night since everyone was trying to sleep, even though it was large. The sound echoed throughout the concrete corridor.

Two ginormous guards blocked their path with large spears. "Where to, kid? You know the rules, there aren't any unfamiliar outsiders allowed in here."

"Hey, you look familiar," the other guard spoke. "Aren't you Sadie's son?"

"Yes, I am. These are my mom's niece and nephew. Don't

worry about them, they're here visiting," Zephyr lied through his teeth, hoping they wouldn't catch on.

"Well, Sadie Indigo never mentioned having extended family." The guards scratched their heads, but then nodded at each other and let them pass without asking any questions.

Zephyr whispered at them, "Don't look back at them, just keep walking. Once we cross the long hallway, we're almost at my house, we just need to turn twice."

Dexter was struggling to keep up with Zephyr. He huffed and puffed, having a hard time making the turns. Clearly exhausted, he collapsed by Zephyr's door.

"Mom, are you here?" Zephyr called out. "Come inside, I don't think she is here. Dexter, you need to rest for a bit. Here is a glass of water. You need it to rehydrate. The both of you can stay in my room. I'll stand guard until mom comes back. I don't want to give her a fright when she sees the two of you. You're going to need this, Dexter, it's bread."

"Where is the ham and cream cheese?" Dexter asked.

Crimson pulled Dexter aside, telling him to stop, that this wasn't his home planet and that Zephyr lived in a different world and in a different time. "We're guests here. Stop being mean, they live differently than we do."

Dexter already knew that, but he couldn't stop his mouth from rambling on. He shook his head. "But you don't understand, Crimson. We clearly went back in time, I'm the present and you're the future."

Crimson told Dexter to get some rest before eating. He eventually agreed and drifted off to sleep after talking to Crimson.

Crimson decided to check on her AIS•C and noticed she only had half of the power remaining. She rose and began thumbing through the book from the cave for how to return home and if there was anything they could do to get Dexter back to his planet.

Zephyr fell asleep in the chair in the kitchen, waiting for his mom to arrive. The night began to come alive. Singing resounded loudly, accompanied by laughing. The raucous sounds rudely awakened Zephyr. He saw his mother standing in the middle of the kitchen, causing him to get off the chair. "Don't be afraid of my new friends, mom. This is Crimson, she looks different but she won't hurt you. Dexter is sleeping in my bed and he is a human like us."

Sadie laughed. "Don't worry, I won't hurt any of you. Where are my manners? My name is Sadie. I am Zephyr's mom, of course you already know that. Well, why don't you go wash up and I'll prepare some food. We can chit chat. Oh, the washroom is outside, that door there takes you to it," Sadie spoke in a bubbly voice.

Crimson looked at Sadie. "Well, I am... different. I don't eat or use the bathroom, I'm not human."

Sadie fanned herself. "Umm, I'm sorry, did you say you are not human? I can see you're different, but in a way, you do look like me."

CHAPTER EIGHT
HAYDEN HARPER

DEXTER STUMBLED GROGGILY out of bed. His hair was a mess like a monster. Rubbing his eyes, he walked out of Zephyr's bedroom. Sadie laughed out loud, quickly covering her mouth.

"The watering hole is outside in the back, you look like you could really use it. The bathroom is out back as well."

Once he entered the bathroom, vertigo took over and he became faint. The sight of a hole in the ground for a toilet stunned him. Dexter panicked, stumbling outside to get some air. Sweat rolled down his face. He took a deep breath and held it. Mustering the courage, he returned to the rudimentary bathroom and relieved himself. The success of doing something on his own made him proud. He knew there was no running water, like a standing sink or soap. Dexter walked towards the well and grabbed the cup that was on the edge of the well. He dipped the cup into the bucket and poured the water onto his hands and did the same for the other hand. But Dexter did not feel like his hands were cleaned enough, so he took out wipes from his knapsack to clean his hands, he also poured water on his messy hair and used the wipe as a comb to straighten his hair.

Zephyr turned his attention towards Crimson. "I know of a cabin in the woods that has been abandoned for years. Eden once told me that it has a brown door and that she's fairly certain no one lives there. The strangest part is that it's located in the deepest, darkest part of the woods, and that scares me... On one side the sun never really shines, we are not sure why."

Everyone gathered their things and Zephyr packed essential supplies for their long journey ahead. Making their way to the front of the village, they could see the guards talking to each other up ahead. Zephyr threw a rock. It skittered across the tiles, making a rattling sound and echoing in the distance.

Being alert, the guards shouted, "Who's there?"

The plan worked well and the guards ran towards the noise's echoes. Crimson, Dexter and Zephyr went out of the same gate where they had entered. They walked towards the lake down the path where Eden and Zephyr had been riding their horse when they had first met Crimson and Dexter.

"Where exactly are you taking us, Zephyr?" asked Dexter.

"Eden told me about a cabin in the woods," said Zephyr.

They kept on walking ahead, passing a thick, lush forest where the autumn leaves had already changed color. They were now orange, yellow and brown. Crimson had never seen leaves changing before, she had only read about it in training camp.

"Is it scary?" Dexter said in a frightened voice.

"No need to be scared, Dexter," said Zephyr.

Dexter's teeth chattered. "Umm, I'm not. Why would you think that, Zephyr?"

The forest became awfully quiet, and it bothered Dexter. He laughed nervously and his eyes darted all around him. Even though it was daytime, there was no light on this side. It seemed the sun could not penetrate the trees here. They saw the darkest path surrounded by the night.

Dexter looked at Zephyr for guidance and Zephyr put his

index finger up to his mouth to shush Dexter. They kept on walking. Zephyr knew they were close. He spotted large banana leaves and palm trees, and he knew that he was in the right area. They parted the banana leaves, and that was where they saw the cabin, still standing in a good condition.

Zephyr opened the cabin door. Surprisingly enough, it was unlocked. Crimson walked in first and made sure that it was safe to stay inside. She signaled to them to let them know it was safe. Zephyr stood by the front door and waved at them.

"Take care, friends. I have to run back home."

"Okay, Zephyr. Take care," said Dexter. Then he started to sweat. "Crimson, I can't see. This cabin is dark."

Crimson shined her light by pressing a button her AIS•C. Dexter became excited when he spotted something familiar.

"There is a fireplace, let's start a fire." Dexter grabbed a stick from the fireplace and pulled a larger wooden board from the wall. He put the stick to the wooden board and started spinning it with his hands.

Dexter got frustrated. "It's too cold in here, I can't do this correctly. The sweat from my hands is making the stick too damp and it isn't working. I can only do this if I have a magnifying glass and some sun. Is that even possible here?" Dexter looked at Crimson. Crimson nodded at Dexter.

"It's okay. I'll shine some light and you'll get the fire going, just calm down and focus."

Crimson found a magnifying glass on a table and handed it to Dexter. She shined the light, magnifying it onto the wooden board. Sure enough, smoke started to rise from the board. A small flame appeared, then sparked out. Dexter gently blew on it, igniting the flames. They moved the wooden board to the fireplace, creating a bigger fire.

Dexter smiled widely. "We did it!"

Crimson shook her head. "No, Dexter, you did it."

Dexter became proud of himself. "I learned from my father. He taught me everything I needed to know."

They explored the cabin, looking for clues. Could it have been someone's house? Crimson's suspicions were confirmed. She found an old book. Flipping through the pages, paragraphs by paragraphs started to appear in front of her. An empty ink well and a quill sat nearby.

Dexter found strange bottles filled with some type of liquid. Each bottle was see-through with different colors. He even found a jar with eyes inside and one with what looked like human hair. There was a bottle with moving smoke inside of it. The strange part of the house was that it didn't have any dust in it. Everything looked new and clean. At this point, his mind ran wild and his imagination raced. "What if a witch lives here?"

It was the only explanation, Dexter thought. Witches were the only ones who had jars of eyes and hair and all kinds of potions. He spotted something near the end table by the bed. It moved a bit. He looked down at his feet and noticed a lever. Dexter kneeled down, grabbing the lever, and gave it a jerk. The end table slid down. Dexter saw a large book and grabbed it. After setting the heavy book on the lever, he walked over, peeked in, and noticed stairs descending. He also saw lit torches. Dexter grew afraid. What – or who – could possibly be down there? He carefully descended downstairs and touched the limestone wall so he wouldn't slip off the stairs since there was no railing. He spotted a huge boulder and began looking at it. He noticed drawings on it.

"Crimson, come here!"

Crimson became concerned and sprinted towards Dexter, thinking that he was in danger. There were all kinds of strange drawings and writings on the cave walls below. Crimson saw a girl accompanied by a man who wore something on his head.

Dexter said, "That is a crown. But who are they?"

Crimson stared at him questioningly. Dexter spotted a girl and a king, as well as something else: a name.

"Crimson, look here. Shine your light so I can read the name better."

Crimson shined her light on the name. Dexter became ecstatic.

"Crimson, it says Eden!"

"Okay, if that is Eden, who is the man next to her?" said Crimson. Dexter studied it some more.

"The man is a king, wearing a crown. It could mean a lot of different things. The message isn't clear as to what Eden is doing next to the man."

There was a knock at the door.

"Stay here, Dexter. I'll see who it is."

Crimson made her way back up the stairs. She opened the door and was greeted by Zephyr. "Zephyr, it's nice to see you here."

Zephyr peeked over her shoulder. "What have you been up to? I see you have the fire going. It looks like a home. Did you find out who used to live here?"

"Dexter believes it's a witch's house," said Crimson.

Dexter yelled their names. Zephyr and Crimson both ran to him. "Dexter, are you okay? What happened?"

"Another man appeared next to Eden in front of my eyes." Dexter was genuinely concerned. Zephyr was confused about what Dexter was talking of. He kneeled on the floor where Dexter was crouched down.

"Look at this cave drawing. This is Eden, and this is a king. Now, right here is another man that just appeared next to Eden," said Dexter.

Zephyr thought to the moment when his mom had told him about the former king of Alaric, named Dimitri. He scratched his head.

Dexter urged, "Well, it looks like her. The drawing has her red hair, orange eyes, and it dresses like her."

Zephyr was confused. "We don't know why a king is right next to her, or who this new man that just appeared is, either. We're making assumptions." Zephyr shivered. "This place gives me the creeps, guys. I think we should get out of here."

There was a rush, like a gust of wind, and the cellar door slammed shut. The suddenness alarmed everyone and they all spun around to look.

"What just happened? Is it just me, or did it just get even colder?" said Dexter.

"Hello, Zephyr," a voice whispered. "I see you found me, but I am not there. Does it surprise you? I still live after all these years. I'm the witch lord Hayden Harper. It's perfect you brought your friends to live in my cabin. I only want you, though. Not your mother Sadie, Eden or your friends."

Zephyr didn't know which direction to look in. "What are you talking about, you creep? What do you mean you're not here? Am I supposed to know you? I couldn't care less if you were alive after all these years. I don't understand any of this. Why would I care who you are?"

"Zephyr, you're very silly. You should at least know about me, everyone here does." The whispering continued around his left ear, causing Zephyr to turn to his left.

"No, not really. No one knows who you are."

"What do you mean no one knows who I am? Of course everyone in the Kingdom of Alaric knows me."

Zephyr's face scrunched up. "There was once a Kingdom of Alaric, but no more. I live in a village called Renu Claw. Now, who is the man beside Eden?"

"Do you really think I am going to tell you? There is something I need in return from you, boy."

Crimson stood firm next to Zephyr. "Zephyr, don't make a deal with this man. We don't know who it is."

"Look, I already told you my name. I'm Hayden Harper, the powerful witch lord."

"Reveal yourself, coward," Zephyr cried.

"No one calls me a coward, you silly child."

A powerful gust of wind pushed both Dexter and Zephyr backward.

"Only cowards are afraid to reveal themselves. Prove to me you aren't one," yelled Crimson. Hayden Harper lashed out with another gust of wind in an attempt to knock her down.

"Your gusts of wind won't knock me down. Can't you tell I am not like you?" Crimson said. Hayden gave up on trying to knock her down.

"To answer your question of who that king is next to the girl, Eden... I can sense she means an awful lot to you. Maybe your girlfriend? Oh, my child, if only you knew the secret lying beneath the truth there. Did you know your mother gave you to me in exchange?"

Zephyr clenched his fists. He was angry since he couldn't see who he was talking to. "That's not true, my mum would never do that to me. She loves me. I swear, if you touch one single strand of my girlfriend's hair, you'll wish you never, ever set foot in this town."

"Oh, I am so scared of you, Zephyr," Hayden mocked. "Don't worry, it's only you I care about. I'm going to collect you soon and there is nothing you or any of your friends can do for you, unless they take you somewhere else to live. Find me and make a deal. I can't guarantee you'll come back alive. Run home and tell your mother about me. Tell her I said hello and that I'll come collect you soon." The echo of Hayden Harper's laughter could be heard before he completely disappeared, causing the fire inside of the torches to flicker.

Crimson sensed Zephyr being distraught. "Wow, this is intense. What are you going to do? You can't possibly believe everything he said."

Zephyr attempted to remain calm. "No, but we need to go back to the village and see what mum says before I believe any of this."

They all ran back upstairs to see if anything in the bookshelves yielded any information. Zephyr wanted to know whether there were any clues as to what Hayden Harper was talking about. The books yielded nothing, just a bunch of random blank sheets. Zephyr threw them to the ground and ran out of the cabin, leaving Crimson and Dexter behind.

Zephyr knocked quietly on the door of his mum's house. She opened the door to find her son staring straight back at her. "Come inside, you silly child. Where are the others?"

Zephyr walked inside. "Mum, what were you doing today? I need to ask you a question."

Sadie pulled a chair to sit. "Yes, ask away, Zephyr."

Zephyr paced around the kitchen. "Who is Hayden Harper? He said he was some witch lord. Mum, can you tell me?"

She got off the chair and a bit of anxiety took over sending hot flashes throughout her body. "Oh, look at this mess. I must clean the house. Zephyr, can you help me? We need to clean, there is so much to do."

He clearly sensed his mum was avoiding his questions, but he didn't give up. "Mum, stop. I really need to know what is going on. I saw Hayden Harper in the darkened forest."

His mother laughed nervously and tried dodging his question. "Zephyr, you know you're not allowed to go there. Look at you, you're running off to places you're not supposed to go to. I'll be going everywhere with you, whether you like it or not, until I learn to trust you again. Then you can go on without me." She wasn't making any sense when she spoke.

"Mum, you're avoiding my questions on purpose. They found a drawing on the cave walls. There was Eden, the king, and all of a sudden the witch lord Hayden Harper appeared in front of us. He told me you had made a deal with him." Zephyr lost his patience with his mother, growing anxious. "I need to know, mom. I am not a child anymore."

Sadie started to cry and fell against the wall, sliding down. She felt ashamed of her response to her son's demanding questions. "Oh, Zephyr, you're right. I can't keep this secret from you. You have to promise me you won't get angry. I want you to know that I was forced into it by Strange Old Woman living next door to us. She took care of you when you were a baby, and she did something to you behind my back. She was the only one who made the unfortunate deal with Hayden Harper. She confessed she did something bad while I was in town. I felt bad for her when she told me the truth about what she did. She was sad and angered because her husband had given her daughter to the king. She confessed this to me.

"She went to the witch lord's cabin and gave you away to him. By the time you turn nineteen, you will join him in return for her to get her daughter back. I was so angered she did it to me. It's like she stabbed me in the heart for trusting her to take care of you. We stopped talking. I am so sorry to keep all this from you, but it was the only way to protect you from everything. I know I have failed you."

Sadie wept more, becoming angered by the thought of Strange Old Woman living next door. Zephyr stared at his mum, speechless. He was seventeen. Soon he'd be gone, not with his beloved Eden. Too soon. It was becoming clear that everything was falling apart. Eden became a distant dream. He could not talk to his own mum any longer. Opening the door, he looked at his mum for the last time, and slammed the door behind him.

Sadie laid down on the floor, her tears coming in torrents. She doubted her son could ever love her after she had hidden the secret for so long. She understood the feeling; she was doing the same thing to Strange Old Woman. The guilt ate at her.

Meanwhile, Zephyr could hear her cries behind the door, but did nothing about it. He felt it was his mum's fault since she was supposed to protect him. She could no longer be trusted.

Sadie eventually got up, moved to the table and found a scrap of paper. She wrote to Zephyr:

Dear Zephyr,

When you find this letter, I won't be here anymore. Seeing you leave has left me completely heartbroken and it aches too much. I love you, Zephyr. Saving you was all I could do. I wish I could have been a better mom to you and that I could have protected you, but I just didn't know how... If I could, I would go back in time and not leave you with that woman. I would have trusted myself to take you with me to the market instead.

- Love, your mum, Sadie

"Always and forever my son." Sadie set the letter on the table, wiping her tears away. She closed the door behind her and made her way to Strange Old Woman's house. She pounded at her front door.

"Sadie! What are you doing here? What a shock to see you here. I hope you aren't still too mad about what I did. Zephyr, oh how handsome he has grown up to be." Strange Old Woman was smitten.

"I am not here to forgive you, I am here to warn you," Sadie said. "I told my son what happened, he didn't take it very well. Now he hates me. He is now seventeen, which makes me cry even more. You know darn well what happens after two years, so I'm leaving. Not being able to ever see him again will break me even more. I trusted you more than anyone in town with the care of my own son. Now he hates me for what I allowed you to do to him. I just can't witness him being taken away."

Sadie stormed off. Strange Old Woman felt terrible for what she had done to Sadie. It tore her heart apart but the emotions didn't hit her at that moment.

Crimson knew she had to invisibly connect with Dexter like they did in the cave, before they left the cabin. Crimson became intensely focused once again. In her mind, she whispered, "Please work, please work..."

An intense breeze went underneath her and around Dexter, causing him to open his eyes. Crimson, too, opened her eyes. They both had big smiles again, They knew that it had worked again.

While they were doing so, they saw Zephyr suspiciously standing almost outside of the entrance.

"Why does Zephyr look suspicious?" said Dexter.

"I don't know, Dexter. Even though he can't see us, let's keep our distance and see what he does next," Crimson said.

All of a sudden, Crimson's AIS•C started beeping. Stopping where they were, she thought she might have run out of battery. Crimson didn't know what to do or how to turn it off. Dexter looked at her acting up and moving all around. "Crimson, what are you doing?"

She panicked. "I need to turn off this beeping sound. Don't you hear it?"

Dexter put his hand on her hands. "Crimson, I don't hear anything."

Crimson became speechless. She was trying her best to ignore the beeping even though the loud sound was getting to her. They walked inside, carefully following Zephyr, even though he couldn't see them.

Crimson became speechless. She was trying her best to ignore the beeping even though the loud sound was getting to her. they walked inside, carefully following Zephyr, even though he couldn't see them. "Hey, look he looks angry, though. I wonder what happened. Too bad we can't ask him, he can't hear us. We can follow and see where he goes?" said Dexter. Too bad we can't ask him, he can't hear us. We can follow and see where he goes?" said Dexter.

Before they could try and follow him, he was stopped.

"Stop!" bellowed the guards. "You're not allowed to go there, Zephyr. You know where you belong, with your mum at home or in the courtyard, nowhere else. We suggest you run back to your mum before something bad happens."

The beeping sound on the AIS•C became even louder. Crimson needed to find whatever she was nearby, but she needed to stay focused on getting Zephyr out first.

"Crimson, it's okay if you need to find where your beeping is leading you to," said Dexter. Crimson agreed with him. They walked away from the guards and Crimson spotted a brown door with a large padlock at the end of a corridor. Her standing there made the beeping grow stronger. "Well, it is getting louder if I stand here. Whatever is behind this door, I need to find out myself. You can't come, Dexter, but we'll help Zephyr first. If it does work then don't let go of my hand, you'll be attached to me and invisible, too."

Dexter picked up a loose rock and they walked towards the guards. He threw the rock far down the corridor. The guards then heard a clanking sound in the nearby distance. "Hey, what was that? Don't move, Zephyr."

The guards were on high alert and ran towards the sound. Both Dexter and Crimson walked back towards Zephyr and once they stopped holding hands, they both became visible again and smiled at him.

"Zephyr, take Dexter with you. I need to do something important here," said Crimson. Now she knew why she had to be on this planet. Crimson was being led to what she was supposed to find.

CHAPTER NINE
CONFLICT AND CANDOR

CRIMSON WALKED RIGHT through the large padlock door, and the ground lights beneath her flickered on. The floor and walls were fully encased in metal. The long, narrow path stretched far, metallic doors all stacked on top of one another. The lighting surrounded the top of the ceiling.

The sense of pressure shifted in the room. She could sense footsteps coming from behind her. Then a man appeared in front of her. A bald, evil-looking young man to be exact. He gave her a cold, blank stare, analyzing her. He took off his long black coat and matching gloves, revealing his identity. Crimson sized him up also, realizing he was almost like her, although he wasn't fully an AI species. His body was completely human, just his left arm wasn't.

The beeping became impossible to ignore. She knew exactly where she was supposed to be.

"First of all, what is that beeping for? I know which questions you're going to ask. Let's get introductions out of the way, you may not have heard of me. The name is Mortimort Montay. Based on the looks of you, you're from Annaecy."

Crimson was shocked and stumbled backwards.

"Wait, you can hear that too? And Annaecy? The forbidden land? I live in Arawn now. Why do you want to know my name? And who are you?"

Mortimort walked closer to Crimson. "Yes, is there a way to turn it off? And you're feisty. Your attitude reminds me of someone familiar, but I am not quite sure about it. But what do you mean forbidden land?"

Crimson replied to Mortimort, "My name is Crimson. I'm not sure, this is the first time I've heard this beeping. But knowing that these AIS•Cs are also used to find things and to help us, the beeping was guiding me to who I needed to find. And that's you, Mortimort. Yes, I did say forbidden land. That's where the louse live, and I live on Arawn."

Mortimort grinned. "Can you touch it? Or press the buttons? See, wasn't difficult, was it? And I had no idea. You may have a lot of questions because I know where you come from. Now I know why I feel such a connection towards you... You're her."

She touched her AIS•C with her palm and the sound stopped. "Why are you here, though? You do know that this is a planet ruled by humans? Which means you're no longer in Annaecy."

Mortimort was taken aback by what he heard. "What do you mean I'm no longer in Annaecy? Not long ago, I discovered these strange structures in an unknown part of Annaecy. I left when the town suddenly turned dark, leaving my fiancé alone. I know, how selfish of me. I came to a realization when I was further away, when the sky wasn't dark anymore and the land was sandy. To my surprise, there was no one guarding these tall structures. I sneaked inside without being seen and I heard something ticking. I didn't know where the sounds were coming from until I saw these small containers. I helped myself to a few for my own personal use without having a clue what they were.

It's like when I had these small containers in my hands, I became someone else. It was unexplainable.

"After a while, I went back to those structures for a second time. I escaped, but it didn't take too long until they spotted me. I thought I could pretend I didn't know where I was, and that's when I felt a pinch strike me from behind. Quickly turning around, I was startled by strange-looking men. They discovered me and introduced themselves as military enforcements and MCOs."

Mortimort kneeled on the ground, begging for his life. The MCOs struck his left arm. By that point he felt like they were going to kill him.

The military enforcements looked at each other. "Stand up, human. We won't hurt you, yet... We want to know how you discovered us."

Mortimort stood up. "Oh, thank you so much. I traveled far and saw those strange structures up there."

The strange men looked at each other and took out long, black batons. The MCOs pressed a button on the sides of their weapons and strong, electric volts came out of them, causing Mortimort to jump back in fear. Putting his hands in front of him, he gulped. "Whoa, whoa, easy there. I mean no harm. I just... just..." He became speechless.

The MCOs struck his left arm and his eyes rolled back, avoiding shrieking in pain when he dropped to his knees. Being the man that he was, he didn't want to express any pain.

By that point he felt like they were going to kill him. Mortimort instantly held out his arm in defense. Breathing heavily, he fainted. The MCOs saw that his flesh was deteriorating and soon enough his bones were starting to disappear.

"Human, wake up."

Nothing came out, but he was still breathing. They moved quickly to repair this human's arm. Releasing tiny mites, they managed to save his arm although they couldn't replicate human flesh.

Soon Mortimort gained their trust, but he was wrong. He was confused why a random shadow had led him there. They soon turned him in to their Highest Commander, blindfolding him. He could hear them talking despite having no idea where they took him. They threw him over the mountains onto the other side and left him there. When he took off the blindfold, it was dark. Unsure where he was, he only had the moonlight for guidance. Mortimort stumbled inside a cave. "Hello? Is anyone here?"

The cave was dark and he saw no one. A shadow darted in and out. He wasn't sure what he was seeing, or if it was even real. Were his eyes playing tricks on him?

"Hello? Is anyone here? I mean no harm."

A shadow walked out in front of him. "Hi, my name is Finder. Who are you? Are you looking for an old book?"

Mortimort was at first confused by a talking shadow that looked like a person.

"Yes, I am looking for an old book."

"Great, follow me." Finder led him where the old book was held in.

"Thank you, Finder, I got it from here."

He was confused why a random shadow had led him there. That part of the cave was darker. He couldn't read the stone book, anyways. He wasn't sure what to even look for. His heart skipped a beat when he heard something beeping. A rumbling sound came from underneath his feet, the ceiling shook uncontrollably and started to crumble. Huge pieces fell on his head, hitting him and knocking him unconscious.

"When I awoke, I was here in this very spot. And I had no idea that I was on another planet until you told me." Mortimort looked at Crimson. "Now I know why your AIS•C beeped." That is where he paused and didn't continue.

Dexter could tell that Zephyr was stressed. "Zephyr, are you okay?"

Zephyr said nothing. Tears streamed down his face and the feeling of guilt rushed throughout his body as the argument he had had with his mum replayed in his mind over and over again. He couldn't shake off the sight of his own mum hurting because he had placed the blame on her instead of seeing her side of the story. All he wanted to do was comfort her, like she had done for him.

While Zephyr was in his feelings, Dexter spotted a letter on the kitchen table and handed it over to him.

Dexter panicked when he heard a knock at the front door. Zephyr went to open the door.

Strange Old Woman looked at Dexter questioningly. "Who are you? I've never seen you around here. Are you new? Zephyr, come to my house, I need to tell you something important."

He followed her into her house and left Dexter behind.

"Zephyr, what are you doing out there all by yourself? Where is your mum?"

"What do you mean where is my mum? Did she leave? Was it my fault she left?" He looked at her in confusion.

"Look, what happened with me and your mum is something I regret deeply. I wish I could take it back, but that's not how life works. I do understand what I did was wrong. All I wanted was to hold my beloved daughter once again," said Strange Old Woman. She lit her lantern while speaking. Zephyr paced around the kitchen, back and forth, his eyes panning to the flame. He recalled the letter Dexter had given him. He pulled it out from his pocket and sat down, reading the message his mum had left for him. He felt the pain in her handwriting. Breaking her porcelain heart made his pain set in stronger. He should have been there for her, not blame her for everything.

"I'm a terrible son. I should leave with Hayden Harper, she'll be happy."

"Don't say that, you're just angry at the moment." Strange Old Woman walked over and put her hands on Zephyr's shoulders. "It's okay, my boy. Your mother should be fine. She told me not to tell you, but she left since she didn't want to cause you more pain. I feel leaving you here wasn't the best option in this situation. After all, she's your mum. The person you should be furious with is me."

His eyes filled with tears as he watched the flames dance around the room. A darkness soon took over his body. Zephyr became possessed by Hayden Harper. "Remove your hands from my shoulders, now!" His demeanor changed, his voice sounded horrifying; a cold, eerie tone. Strange Old Woman was startled, catching a glimpse of evil within his eyes. She clutched her hands to her chest and started breathing heavily.

"Because of what you did to me and my mum, Hayden Harper returns to seek his long-awaited prize... me. Does that make you happy?" Zephyr screamed.

She had thought she wouldn't even be alive to experience this moment when her deal had come to light. Being alive this long, she knew this was the evil work of none other than

Hayden Harper. He wanted to see her alive, not getting off so easily.

Zephyr felt lightheaded, stumbling and rubbing his eyes. Seeing the sheer horror on Strange Old Woman's face caused him to run out.

"Help, someone help me!" Her plea for help fell quiet as her voice was much too fragile to be heard. She noticed the lantern was almost out. She was startled by an ominous figure moving towards her. Knowing full well she deserved nothing, she thought she was hallucinating. A feeling like a heavy presence pressed down on her. An intense chill washed over her, and then he appeared before her eyes.

"Surprise, remember me? I'm letting you feel your age for the first time, do you like it? You'll be reunited with your daughter soon, but just as you're about to finally have her, I'll snap my fingers, absorbing your helpless soul away. All that remains is your dying body. Soon enough, your daughter's eyes will fill with sadness. A happy reunion devolved into a devastating end."

She felt a forceful wind stand her up from behind. Strange Old Woman was frightened to hear from Hayden Harper that everything was going to change soon.

"Before I leave, there is one last thing I should tell you. Zephyr knows where your daughter is." Evil laughter faded from the room.

Zephyr no longer wanted to be selfish, only thinking about himself. He knew it was his duty to return to the others, especially his beloved Eden. Dexter and Zephyr met up with Crimson and went to see Eden. She was waiting by their usual spot by the pond.

Eden kneeled down. "Zephyr, release anything holding you

back. I don't like seeing you like this. It's okay, let it go. I'll always love you, no matter what you tell me."

"Zephyr, you can tell her the truth," Dexter urged. "You must tell her the truth already."

Eden's tears streamed down her face. "What truth is Dexter talking about? I agree with him, stop protecting me."

Zephyr kneeled in front of her, taking her hand. He tried his best to be strong for her. Instead, he cried. He didn't want to show weakness in front of her, but all the pent-up emotions became too much, and he let the tears flow. "My love, everything will be okay. I won't ever let anything bad happen to you."

"My heart would break in an instant, shattering into millions of pieces if you don't tell me what Dexter wants you to tell me. My love for you isn't replaceable. Is there something you're not telling me? It's okay, you can tell me, I trust and believe you."

Before Zephyr could say anything else, a roaring, darkened sky appeared above them. A ripping sound took over as strong winds arose, and the tall grass in the distance blew with the wind. Subtle, red flashes lit up the sky, and out of nowhere, it was as if nothing had ever happened. Everything returned to normal.

Only Eden showed discomfort toward what they had just experienced. "I'm sorry, Zephyr, I must get home before it gets too late or else my father will get angry at me and will no longer let me outside. I wouldn't know what to do if that were to happen." Eden leaned over and gave Zephyr a soft kiss on the cheek. She whispered in his ear, "Whatever you're going through, trust me. Tell me and I'll be here whenever you're ready."

The sky became dark again, then red flashes lit up the darkness once more. Eden ran barefoot through the tall grass. Racing all the way home as quick as she could, she hoped her father wouldn't be angry at her. She disliked that her father lost his temper if she was even a second late. Time was against her. Seeing the log cabin up ahead, she knew she was almost home. Once she got there, she noticed her father's friends were standing at the front door.

Eden often wondered who the people surrounding her father were. He would always tell her they were friends and that she shouldn't worry too much about it. Stubbornly, Eden only grew more suspicious of them when they came over at all times of the night. She felt disgust every time they came over, and at the way they stared at her as she passed.

"Eden Marie Alaric, get inside, now. Do you know how late it is? If you haven't noticed, there is about to be a storm and I want to talk about where you have been all day."

Eden looked at her father nervously. She rushed to her bedroom which was adjacent to the porch. Her curiosity had grown and she was old enough to know about her father. Why was he keeping secrets from her? She carefully listened through the thin cabin wall.

"Rumor has it that the witch lord Hayden Harper returned and is looking for that boy."

A loud heckling accompanied by a roar of laughter erupted among the men. "Aren't you worried he might come looking for you? After what you did?" The laughing continued.

"Nope, I don't believe the witch lord Hayden Harper is going to come for me. That revenge goes to the boy, his mum, the old man and the old woman. My girl and I are going to be okay."

Emotions washed over Eden as she grappled with what to do. With the information she had just heard spoken by the men and her father, she wanted to know who Hayden Harper was. What boy did they speak of? She felt she barely knew her father. He hadn't spoken much about this part of his life. He never spoke about anything. Had Eden ever had a mother? Her father made excuses every time she asked questions. He went from hot to cold and started yelling for her to mind her own business, rambling about how she appreciated nothing he ever did for her. She told herself he didn't mean it when he told her she could leave his house if she didn't approve of his rules. No longer a child, her concern was piqued by his silence and the conversation she had just overheard. It confirmed much of what she suspected.

"Eden, get out here, now," Dimitri yelled. "You're going to tell me exactly where you were or else bad things will happen. So, where were you? And this time, your lovely smile won't help you."

Eden looked up, meeting his gaze. His eyes were filled with rage she'd never seen before. She felt she had to come up with the best excuse to give to her father to maintain the secrecy of her relationship with Zephyr. "I went to visit Ms. Natasha Baker, you know, she's a fragile woman. I wanted to help her. She needed me to pick up some food at the market."

He sat quietly for a brief moment, but couldn't find a reason to doubt her. Knowing how he acted, he was surprised Eden took the time to help the poor, the sick and the elderly. It was something he had refused to do as a king. In the end, it was her goodness of heart that made him have a soft spot for her. Although he was protective of Eden, he couldn't become over-bearing of her. He stood up from his rocking chair. "You know that I don't like you going to the market all alone. Especially in Renu Claw. I prefer you go to the market in the castle, instead of the market in the small village. Alright, run along."

"Yes, sir. Thank you, father." She recognized he was letting her go outside after dark. She took full advantage of it, running to get away from her father's friends and from his sight. She never understood why he had such a problem with her going to the market in the small village. Was there something that he didn't want her to find out?

Pulsating flashes of red light appeared in the sky before her, and a swirling wind gradually surrounded her. She could no longer see what was in front of her. The loud sound of the wind irritated not just her eyes; the pattern of the winds was making her nauseated. She was stuck and couldn't get out.

"Where am I? I think I'm lost," Eden yelled. She heard another voice. Turning around, she spoke quietly, "Hello? Who is there? Is someone there?" She knew there wasn't anyone else with her, but then she felt something grab her from behind. Eden shrieked, letting out a scream before whoever it was had a chance to cover her mouth.

"You stupid child. Why did you let out a scream? I will have to take you beneath the darkness. Zephyr will have to rescue you. Can't wait to see your father's expression when he finds out his beloved daughter is missing."

Eden struggled. "Are you the witch lord Hayden Harper?"

"How do you know of me? Your father finally told you? Or should I say the one who stole you away from your real parents?"

"Lies, that's not true! Why would my own father need to steal me? I am his daughter. I am not a child anymore, so if you're going to take me away, do it. What is stopping you?"

"No, child, you are not his daughter."

"You may be powerful, but what you say about my father isn't true. I know he's a good man at times."

"You silly little girl, you have no idea who your father really is, do you? There are too many secrets to be told and there is a reason your father hasn't told you anything."

Hayden Harper took Eden and disappeared into the endless darkness of the land, taking the swirl of wind away. The sky cleared and the red lights vanished.

. . .

"Hey, what were all those flashing red lights? Did anyone hear a girl screaming?"

Crimson turned to Dexter. "What scream, Dexter? We didn't hear a girl screaming."

Zephyr's heart was pulling at him. "I can't explain it, but I can feel something is wrong with Eden. It's the love that brings two people close to each other. Love is a strong feeling, no matter how far they are from each other."

"The love you speak of is a strong connection," Crimson said.

"Yes, Crimson, that is correct. Eden is in trouble. I must find her."

CHAPTER TEN
THE FINAL FIGHT

CRIMSON STOPPED Zephyr from making a mistake at Eden's father's cabin. "Easy, Zephyr. You don't know where she is. She could be anywhere by now and I know she isn't with her father. You're going to stay right here until we have a plan."

"I know who might have her and you'll not like it: Hayden Harper."

"Let's think this through first before we jump to conclusions. Zephyr, do you know who Eden's father is?"

"Yes and no. All I know is that he isn't well liked in the village, although he lives far. We must be careful. He is known to have a bad temper."

"Well, who is going to go first? Me, Dexter, or Zephyr?"

Dexter mustered up the courage to go knock on the front door.

"Who goes there?" an abrasive, loud male voice rippled from the house. A bearded man of huge stature opened the door.

"My name is Dexter and these are my friends, Zephyr and Crimson. We know you don't know us, but we know your daughter, Eden."

"What did she do this time? Did she get herself in trouble again?" He could smell the fear on them.

"No, sir. Eden is a sweet, kind and lovely girl. She gets herself in no trouble, sir." Dexter smiled nervously.

"Is there a reason you knocked on my door? You better have a good reason to do that."

Crimson quickly interrupted, "We just wanted to inquire about your daughter. We have reason to believe she isn't here. As her father, you should be more concerned about her."

"Eden's father, do you know where your daughter is?" Dexter inquired nervously.

Dimitri growled, "First of all, my name isn't Eden's father, it is Dimitri Alaric, and no, I don't know where that girl is. Half the time, I don't even know what she gets herself into."

Shaken, Zephyr stepped before Dimitri. "Excuse me, sir? But did you say Dimitri Alaric? Were you the king of Alaric? My mom Sadie told me all about you. Strange Old Woman lived in the kingdom. Answer me, I know you know who I speak of," he said.

"Why do you ask? Why do you care who I am?" yelled Dimitri.

"Look, I know you are Dimitri Alaric, King of Alaric." Zephyr was scared but showed no fear.

"You're correct," Dimitri responded. "I am Dimitri Alaric, the king of Alaric, and I know of Strange Old Man and his wife."

Zephyr had the information he needed. "Sorry to have bothered you, sir. If we hear anything from her, we'll bring her back here so you don't have to worry about her."

Dimitri sneered at them and slammed the door shut in their faces.

His visitors' mannerism aggravated Dimitri. He became enraged towards them. The feeling of frustration became uncomfortable. He raged and kicked whatever was in front of him. What felt like a liberation from all the pent-up frustration soon turned to carelessness. When Eden or his friends weren't around, his inner demons came out and his guilt started to speak deep inside of him.

He couldn't care less about them finding out the truth about him. It was too much to keep inside after all these years, there was no point in hiding everything. In the end, it all stacked up against him. He hid mainly because of his fears. His demons had kept his secrets, promoting his own, selfish gains. Even though he wanted the truth to come out, he still wanted to live his fantasy of having a daughter while pretending that his wife was still beside him. But he couldn't keep this in any longer, his health was declining faster due to the stress and he didn't sleep well at all.

Maybe one day Eden could forgive him, but she would find out the truth about him regardless. There was still a part of him that would deny everything just to be able to hug her one last time, even if it was just a few seconds. Once she discovered the truth about him, she would forever hate him for everything he stood for. Knowing she may no longer care for him hurt more than life. When that day came, he would see her cast her anger towards him, but that was what he deserved for taking her from her real parents. It was his fault she was suffering, and he could never tell her the truth himself.

They walked through the tall grass to get back to the forest. Straight away, the sky above became pitch-black. A howling noise erupted. Eden's scream echoed and, soon enough, took over. The wind increased, surrounding them in a strong, circular motion that formed a vortex above them. The strength of the wind blindsided Zephyr and Dexter. They were unable to shield their eyes any longer from the dust. It sucked them into a pit of darkness.

Zephyr couldn't see what was in front of him. His stomach tightened and he hit the ground softly, slowly sinking in. He wasn't sure where he was. It was pitch-black, and his eyes had a difficult time adjusting to the darkness. Although he couldn't see, he could feel a wet, icky goo with his hands.

"Dexter, are you here? It's awfully dark, it would be great if you were here."

He didn't get a response back. He attempted to move his feet but couldn't free himself. His neck started aching, but he didn't desire to lay his face in this goo. Tears rolled from his eyes and he was beset with hopelessness.

"If you want to save your friends, you have to surrender."

Crimson recognized the voice in the wind. "Well, I don't have a choice but to surrender. Okay, Hayden Harper, you win."

The wind stopped and Crimson vanished into thin air. Her fall slowed. She hovered in the air, activating her AIS•C. Beams of blue lasers illuminated all at once, creating a bridge towards the end of the darkened cave. She was learning what all her AIS•C could do without the help of the military enforcements and their teachings. She shined her light, instantly spotting Zephyr. She hovered over to him and pulled him from the sticky goo, carefully lowering him onto the bridge. He looked all around his surroundings and realized they were inside a dark cave without any opening at the top of the mountain.

"Zephyr, are you okay?" asked Crimson.

"Ugh, I think so. I'm sticky and it feels so heavy." Zephyr struggled to get up. "Okay, we should really get going."

Crimson spotted a large, black steel door emitting scattered red lights. She also examined a large amount of beveled numbers covering the door. Before approaching it, she surveyed the surrounding area, scanning the door again to ensure it was okay to enter.

"What is that, Crimson?"

"The numbers are actually ciphers, it's supposed to form a word." Carefully analyzing the door, she recorded and high-lighted everything. It said, 415 251521 2311420 452420518 1144 545 14. DO YOU WANT DEXTER AND EDEN?

A grinding metallic sound rippled in the cave and the door opened before them by itself. Behind the door stood Hayden Harper, and within his grasp were Dexter and Eden. Watching Eden struggle to get away angered Zephyr. He was more deter-mined to rescue his beloved, but at the same time he felt weak, struggling to save her.

Crimson blocked Zephyr's way before he could get to Eden. "Don't go over there, it's exactly what Hayden Harper wants."

"Follow me, boy, you'll get your beloved and this other one."

Ignoring Crimson's pleas, Zephyr saw no choice but to follow Hayden.

"All of this could have been avoided," Hayden Harper bellowed.

"I will never join you, witch lord Hayden Harper," screamed Zephyr.

"We'll see about that." Hayden Harper grinned. He vanished before them and the mountain disappeared slowly. They were back in the middle of Renu Claw.

"Eden, we must take you back home. You will be safer with your father," said Zephyr.

"No, Zephyr. I refuse to leave. Stop protecting me, I am not a child anymore. How many times do I have to repeat myself?"

"What is best for Eden isn't going back to her father. Did you see how he acted when we went to see him?" said Crimson.

"I agree with Crimson. Eden is safer with us, since Eden's father is the king of Alaric, or was. Wait, did I say that out loud? Oops," Dexter blabbed.

Eden quickly turned to Dexter. "What?"

Dexter laughed nervously. "What I meant to say was... sorry, I was thinking out loud and didn't mean to say anything."

"Tell me the truth about my father," Eden urged.

Dexter took a deep breath. "Eden, your father is, or was, the king of Alaric."

"No lies, Dexter. Tell me the truth. You lie. I know my father." Eden covered her ears. Zephyr uncovered them.

"My love, what Dexter says is the truth about your father. He was a king of a town called Alaric, before Renu Claw. My mum told me everything and we went to find your father. He confirmed everything. At first, I didn't want to believe it, either."

Eden was still processing what her beloved told her. She simply didn't want to understand. "Where do we go next, Zephyr? We're most likely in Hayden Harper's lair."

They didn't have much choice but to stay there until Hayden made a move. Crimson turned to Eden. "What do you know about your father, Eden, if I may ask?"

Eden became uncomfortable. "Honestly, very little. He keeps to himself, often confusing me with someone else. He would go on a tirade in his mind, speaking of ruling and being in control. Not only that, he would suddenly stop, stare at the wall for hours, then go outside. I often wonder what happens in his head. I wonder if he's still all there."

They all felt a strong tug on their arms and were dropped one by one back into the forest. There they saw Dimitri, Strange

Old Man, Strange Old Woman, Sadie, Dexter and Eden being held by Hayden Harper.

"If you want your beloved, Zephyr, you'll have to join me," Hayden ordered, not leaving Zephyr much choice. He needed to sacrifice himself. Hayden laughed.

"I could take you anytime, but it would be too easy. I'll just have fun with your feelings, it's fun to see the strong cry," Hayden mocked.

Sadie ran to her son, breaking down, sobbing. "No, my son, don't do it. He just can't take you."

Hayden Harper was excited watching them. Crimson couldn't handle the situation. She drew out burning circles underneath Hayden Harper's legs, slowly crawling up to his body. An intense heat from the circles burned Hayden's thick skin. Screaming in pain and grabbing his chest, he challenged, "How dare you?" Already feeling embarrassed and defeated, he couldn't do anything but disappear.

"Come on, Hayden, show yourself. Don't tell me you're scared of my friend? Play with someone on your own level," yelled Zephyr. He became distraught, dropping to his knees, tears ran down his face.

Dimitri headed to Strange Old Man. "Well, well, well. We meet again, see how much things have changed? Do you see the lovely, sweet young lady over there? Look how much she has grown, soon enough she'll be a woman. Too bad you won't ever get the chance to meet her. She's within reaching distance, much closer than you think."

Strange Old Woman simply gasped as tears ran down her cheeks. "What is her name?"

"Eden Marie is her name. That is the name my beloved wife and I would have given our own daughter if we had a baby girl one day."

Dimitri yanked Strange Old Man's arm harshly, but Crimson intervened.

"This isn't your battle to fight, go away," said Dimitri rudely.

Crimson stood in front of Strange Old Man. "When I see danger, I react, doing everything to help whether you like it or not. Besides, he isn't doing anything to hurt you."

Eden heard the commotion and ran to her father. "Father, what is going on? And why are you hurting this fragile old man? You're the bigger person in all of this. Let go of him, right now."

"Eden, wait," said Strange Old Woman tenderly. Eden's ears perked up as she turned around to smile at the woman. Her voice sounded like a delicate flower. It attracted her to the voice, the almost motherly, soothing and sincere voice. Dimitri lost his mind and attempted to push Strange Old Woman out of the way. Instead, Crimson gently pushed him away from Eden.

A woman wearing a long, white dress with a long veil intervened, tapping Dimitri on the shoulder. He turned around and dropped to his knees. Was it real? Were his eyes deceiving him? His eyes fill with tears. It had to be the work of Hayden Harper, once again attempting to strike a deal with him. But he wanted to believe it was his wife. Eden was surprised to see her father cry, it was the first time ever.

Dimitri pleaded, "My queen, is that you? Or another one of Hayden Harper's tricks to fool me into striking a worthless deal with him? It was never my intention to strike any deals with Strange Old Man, please forgive me, my love."

Katherine didn't want to be deceived by her husband's actions. She held a grudge deep inside of her, but she also wanted to capture that love that had once existed between the two before Hayden Harper had taken her away all those years ago.

She touched his chin gently. "No, you have nothing to worry

about. It's no trick, my love. Hayden Harper came to find me in the kingdom and told me I played an important part in his game. After he captured me, he said we would all be reunited once again and he'd let me be free, but I knew something was up. He kept telling me 'soon dear, soon,' and I've waited years for this moment to come. When he finally said it was time and the game was over, I was overjoyed and grateful this day was here. I was free and excited to join you once again," spoke Katherine.

"My love, if I may? I lost my kingdom looking for you. My loyal men have been by my side ever since. But darkness consumed me as Hayden led me to believe you were dead. I wasn't going to let your death be in vain. We no longer live in the Kingdom of Alaric, we now live in Renu Claw. This is Crimson, she's from the future, she was sent here to help us."

Crimson walked closer to Dimitri. Katherine thanked Crimson for her bravery and looked into Dimitri's eyes. "You didn't lose the kingdom. We don't need an actual location for our kingdom, it lies in our hearts forever."

Dimitri kneeled down and placed his hands on her pregnant stomach.

"Now, I know what you did to Eden and her parents. You must do the right thing now so that your heart will no longer be in the darkness. I am here with you. You must let go of Eden. She needs to be with her real parents. It's better to be in harmony with oneself than in anger. I don't understand why you took someone else's daughter, but I see she changed something in you, even if you don't show it often. She ignited your ability to love again," Katherine spoke in a loving way.

Dimitri bowed to his queen and looked toward Eden, then he spoke, "Eden, I hope you find it within you to forgive me one day. I am truly sorry for taking you away from your parents. Strange Old Woman, it was never my intention to take your daughter. So please, forgive me, and Strange Old Man, forgive me as well. Sorry to bring harm to you."

"Although it's been many years, and we aren't on the best terms, we have come to the conclusion that we can no longer hold a grudge against you. You gave our daughter a home. She knows how to stand up for herself and others. She's everything we ever wanted to have. Thank you, Dimitri."

Dimitri turned to look at his beloved wife. "Are we ready to go, my love?"

Katherine smiled at her husband and they walked away together. After they had left, Hayden Harper exaggerated his clapping, becoming aggressively loud. A high-pitched, evil laughter resounded when he stepped out from the shadows. "Sorry to ruin this happy family reunion, but I'm glad the truth was finally revealed. If anyone is planning to forgive the former king of Alaric, I suggest Eden and Zephyr have the right to know the whole truth." Dumbfounded, Hayden looked all around him. "Where did he go?"

"You're a tad bit late for getting your revenge on Dimitri," said Eden.

Hayden Harper snarled. "We'll forget about him. Eden, your own mother here made a deal with me because she missed you. She gave Zephyr's soul to me once he turns of age."

Eden gigged softly. "Your names couldn't possibly be strange old man and woman."

"You're correct, Eden. My name is Justine and your father's name is Henry."

Justine walked toward Hayden Harper. Henry tried to stop her, but she glared at him and he let go of her. "Take me instead, Hayden. I'm the one who wanted my daughter back in exchange for Zephyr. Even though I saw him as a son, I was being selfish when I saw my best friend Sadie have her child while I didn't have mine."

Tears streamed down Eden's face. She ran to her mum and they embraced each other.

"It's okay, my baby, only a mum's real love can understand how much you truly love Zephyr. I am sorry I did this to both Sadie's son and to my best friend. My anger lies on Henry, my husband, who caused my rage. I ended up breaking Sadie's trust and deserve to face the consequences of my actions. I want you to look at me now, clear those tears and remember, I'll always look after you. Look towards the ocean and the sunset, your lovely eyes are my sunset and Zephyr's lovely eyes are my ocean. I'll be there when you need me. Sadie, please forgive me. Don't be mad any longer, for the sake of our children. I still cherish the happy moments we shared together."

Sadie's legs weakened. She was on the verge of tearing up. In a split second, she and Justine were locked in a hug.

"No, no, don't worry, Justine. I won't let you leave, please stay. Hayden Harper, do your worst and take me instead."

Sadie grabbed Justine's hand and held it tightly. "I regret everything I ever said to you in that moment. I was angry at you when I found out the truth about your plans, Justine. It's been far too long and I can no longer hold onto this grudge against you. I forgive you and always cherish our memories together."

Hayden Harper sneered, glaring at everyone in the room. "Truths are finally coming out. There isn't any real excitement going on, but I'll make it worth it. Are there any last words for Justine or Sadie before I take them away? And yes, I decided they'll both vanish with me."

"I do," an unfamiliar voice spoke out of nowhere.

"Who is there? Reveal yourself."

The stranger stepped in front of Hayden. Crimson couldn't believe who it was.

"You don't know me, my name is Mortimort. I live in the

underground depths of Renu Claw. It may come as a surprise to everyone here."

Crimson looked at him and wondered how he had been able to escape the underground bunker he had been trapped inside of. She ultimately figured out that if she was able to roam freely as an AI, then he could as well, and it had been only a matter of time.

"And do I care who you are? No, shoo, I couldn't care less. Justine and Sadie are still leaving with me. One for summoning me and the other for being the mother of my future ruler. One day, I'll get revenge and rule all of Renu Claw," Hayden Harper laughed. A well calculated move and Hayden's hand grabbed Justine's, trying to pin her down. But Justine lost her balance, falling into Sadie's hands.

"Hayden Harper, you'll know me soon enough." Mortimort activated three AIS•Cs and lasers rapidly generated from them, molding onto Hayden Harper's body. They targeted his ears, hair, arms, legs, and constricted him tighter as he desperately tried to get away. Every attempt at trying to vanish only made him weaker until he fell to the ground.

"Why isn't this working?" asked Hayden Harper.

Mortimort laughed aloud. "I am stronger than you, we are not alike. All you're doing is decreasing your energy, can't you tell? For someone calling himself a witch lord, you're not accustomed to being weak."

Hayden Harper became smitten. "I have no concept of being weak. Come on, great one, we are both evil. We could do so much more as evil meets evil. Now I see it all, a bright future. You and I destroying Renu Claw or ruling it, whatever you like."

Mortimort grinned. "I have a better plan, watch and wait."

He pushed his power to the max. The heat from the lasers became much more intense, causing the laser to become so bright it made it difficult to see. Everyone ducked, shielding their eyes. Once the bright light had dissipated, so had Hayden Harper and Mortimort.

Everyone rejoiced, finding themselves back in Renu Claw. Eden hugged her parents, Sadie hugged her son. Dexter loved the happy reunions of all families.

"Henry, Justine, Mum and Dad, why were you known as Strange Old Man and Strange Old Woman?"

"As for our names, well, when we lived in the Kingdom of Alaric, we were seen as strange. We were judged because we were the older couple there. People always found it strange that we had a daughter at our age. It sort of stuck from there on. But in reality, Hayden's curse made us older than our actual ages. In a way, we are still cursed because we're both older."

Eden laughed gently. "Learning why people called you that, it all seems so silly."

Eden had a sweet, lovely and forgiving nature; she forgave Dimitri even though he wasn't there anymore.

CHAPTER ELEVEN
BACK HOME

EARLY THE NEXT MORNING, it was time to figure out how to return home. Crimson felt like she had failed in getting Dexter back home. Dexter, Zephyr, Eden, Justine, Henry and Sadie all sat at the table to eat bread while Crimson studied the magical book in Zephyr's room. She was uncertain if this book even held the answers she was looking for. Taking the magnifying glass out of the book made words appear.

> *"Speak these words out loud. Those who traveled together on their journey must part ways. Those who live on the same planet will stay together. Whatever you have learned along the way, keep it to yourself and never speak of the other planets that you have discovered, the people that you have met, or the new customs that you may have learned. Secrecy is meant to become a form of protection."*

Dexter walked in after finishing eating and saw Crimson reading the book. She looked at him. "We must say these words on the book out loud."

Dexter went over and read them to himself at first. Crimson and Dexter had to say goodbye to Eden, Zephyr and their families. Eden sighed, knowing it was time, but they didn't want to.

"We will miss you. Though at times, I didn't know what Dexter was talking about," said Zephyr.

Dexter started to cry. "Thank you for sharing a piece of your lives, Eden and Zephyr. I've learned about families, the meaning of friendship, and how humans lived their lives before the future."

Zephyr laughed. "Even though it was a short stay, I've learned a lot about the future and how it's not fun. I would still rather be here on Renu Claw with my mum and Eden."

Eden agreed with Zephyr and laughed. "Good luck on your journey home," she said softly, holding back tears.

Crimson turned to Dexter. "Goodbye, Dexter. It was great meeting you and great having you at my mother's, even though at first I wasn't too thrilled about it. It grew on me to have you there and now here."

Dexter struggled to fight off his tears, being overwhelmed by all the people that he had to leave behind and say goodbye to. "Goodbye, everyone. I'll miss each and every single one of you. Thank you, Crimson, for putting up with me."

Even though goodbyes were already difficult for everyone, Zephyr and Eden taught Crimson how to give hugs gently.

Crimson and Dexter stood together and spoke the words on the book out loud.

"Speak these words out loud. Those who traveled together on their journey must part ways. Those who live on the same planet will stay together. Whatever you have learned along the way, keep it to yourself and never speak of the other planets that you have discovered, the people that you have met, or the new customs that you may have learned. Secrecy is meant to become a form of protection."

Crimson returned to her last known location, which was inside the cave where her journey had first started. She was surprised that it didn't alert the military enforcements of her arrival.

Five miles in, she heard a familiar voice near her. "Wait, it's me, Finder. Did you miss me? Where did Dexter go?"

"Finder." As soon as Crimson said his name, she remembered that Mortimort had said a shadow talked to him. "Finder, I need you to tell me the truth."

Finder looked at her, concerned.

"When you were in your shadow form, did you see a tall man and did you tell him about the book?"

Finder snapped. "I get a lot of visitors around here."

Crimson looked at him. "Seriously, Finder? No wonder every AI species has different stories about coming here and even Asuma had an important map in his shop torn out from the book. How did he know how to transform the book into a regular book? Do you have any idea how much danger your actions may have caused? Mortimort isn't fully an AI. But he is half human and half AI, and he wasn't even searching for the book. You told him about the book and the great part is, instead of landing on another planet, he was taken to an underground area where he had to remain for a long while. Surprisingly enough, he has been kept alive. I don't know how, but something in my AIS•C directed me to go find him. I also need to return the book because somehow it traveled with me. The last thing that we both need is for the MCOs or anyone else to discover this book or anything else in here."

Finder touched his elbow and lowered his head. "Sorry, Crimson. I didn't know that the AI and humans that entered weren't always friendly. I needed a friend or someone to talk to and I thought that everyone who entered were friendly.

Now I know who to trust and who not to trust. The last time you were here, the Entitylst Soldiers updated their security. Let's see if we can pass it again. It's their fault that they lost the book, but good thing you have it, Crimson. What I don't get is why the book went with you, and who does it belong to?"

Crimson followed Finder to find the secret door once again. Finder looked all around him. "Okay, we are here. Be quiet and look around. The Entitylst Soldiers are still here, we don't want any other accidents to happen."

Crimson took out the book. Opening it, she noticed there was a light that flashed three times. She knew this looked familiar. It was in morse code. She wondered why. Was she supposed to discover something? A series of code lined the walls and started to move, forming a sentence. It read as followed, "Must follow the instructions correctly. A hidden clue will be shown to you and the portal door will open."

129519 1144 2589144 205195 2085. LIES THE BEHIND THESE CAVE THE.

"Okay, those are just random words. I can't seem to form a sentence out of them. Now I am starting to wonder what the numbers are supposed to mean. I guess it's starting to mess with me because of the random order."

The random words disappeared, one letter after another. A series of code started to appear again. 2085 1497820 2391212 611212 14144 2085 131518149147 2391212 189195 2589144 205195 31225 231121219 129519 2085 201821208. THE NIGHT WILL FALL AND THE MORNING WILL RISE BEHIND THESE CAVE WALLS LIES THE TRUTH.

"I feel like it's a riddle." Crimson walked around for a bit, taking a step forward and then to the middle. The riddle instructed the night would fall and soon afterwards morning would rise. "That worked, but I don't think it was supposed to happen," she said.

"But it seemed to work, how did you know to go to the middle, Crimson?"

Crimson focused. "I remember when an eclipse occurs, both the sun and the moon align, meeting in the center."

The walls around them shook and another code appeared on the outer walls. Finder gasped in surprise. "That's impossible, the outside can be seen from the inside."

"In unexplored lands, anything is possible, Finder. Nothing is impossible here," said Crimson.

Six holes appeared in the ground. Finder approached to see what was inside the holes, realizing they weren't black voids. A code appeared in front of their eyes in the middle of the portal. Crimson felt proud of herself for getting to apply what she had learned being with Dexter.

25 1231185 156 2085 381147519 920 919 141520 238120 920 19551319. BE AWARE OF THE CHANGES IT IS NOT WHAT IT SEEMS.

"I think I get it, but it sounds confusing. Can you explain that part to me? What is it trying to say, Finder?" Crimson asked.

"Sure thing, Crimson. It means whatever changed is not the reality," said Finder. But it still didn't make sense to her. The ground below them shook for what felt like the longest time, creating small cracks and frightening Finder. He ran to hide in the shadows.

A woman materialized in front of Crimson. Her hair was long, brown and perfectly straightened, she wore a long Kalasiris linen dress and gold bracelets on both of her arms.

"Don't be afraid, my name is Rhinedd and I mean no harm. I need you to trust me."

She heard someone coughing and that was when she saw a

scrawny, thin human stumbling out of nowhere. Before Crimson had a chance to speak out, Rhinedd rushed over to him. "Let me analyze him. He might be dangerous to us."

Crimson panicked, thinking Rhinedd might hurt him. "Wait, don't hurt him, he is my friend. He was outcast as a young boy, he has been forced to live underground in the cave because the Zectic Entitylst Soldier Species said he didn't look like them. He has helped me during my journey and he knows how to speak the Zectic language. Finder is smart, friendly, fast – you should see him run – and he knows what he is talking about."

Rhinedd shooed Finder with her arms. "You say that you're one of us, the Entitylst, and speak our language. I highly doubt that."

Finder had had enough of Rhinedd's attitude. "You may doubt me all you want. I am really getting close to what you're hiding. Are you frightened that I might figure it out? Does it scare you or raise a cause for concern?"

"That's enough, child," Rhinedd said. "You know nothing about me. I don't have a weakness, but you do and I can sense it. You still haven't healed your wounds from being abandoned by your parents, have you? You're like a beacon that I can spot from a mile away."

Finder got closer to Rhinedd. "I may be a child, but I can spot your beacon from a mile away, as well. The anger in your voice showed me everything. The way your speech cracks has shown me that you're one who's hurt, too. Hurt by what? Either by someone you once loved, or then something happened, am I correct? Or are you going to dismiss me because I am simply a child and should know better and just be quiet? Would that please you better?"

Rhinedd screamed at Finder, "Who do you think you are? Coming to my world and telling me what I should feel?"

Finder kept his firm stature. "You know that I'm closer to finding out the truth, and that is why you're trying to confuse me. Just say it already, nothing bad will happen."

Rhinedd lifted up her hand, facing Finder. "I've had enough of you."

"Do it, then. Attack me." Finder stood his ground firmly while staring at her hand.

Crimson stopped Rhinedd. "Stop it, he's friendly."

Rhinedd was clearly flustered. She put her hand back down by her side. "Even if I wanted to, I couldn't. And you're right, I am hiding something... a dark secret. In due time, I'll let you know what it is."

Crimson took out the book. "Here you go, Rhinedd. I need you to keep the book safe."

Rhinedd looked concerned. "Why do you have my book?"

Crimson shook her head. "This book chose me when I went down the portal. Is that why I was supposed to crack the cipher? For you to show up?"

"Impossible! Why did the book pick you? You need to keep it if it chose you. Yes, of course! It was all part of my plan, and it worked."

Crimson still gave the book to Rhinedd as she was worried about the MCOs finding it.

"Hurry back fast, I can only keep this book with me for a little while," Rhinedd said.

"With Crimson gone, can you open the book?" asked Finder.

"No, Finder, I cannot access the book as I am not the chosen one. Without Crimson, it's considered useless to me, to us."

As soon as Crimson walked out of the cave, she was transported right back to the Military Enforcement Soldier Species Home Base. She was met by the Major Commanding Officials and by the High Commanding Officers.

"Well, well, well, what do we have here? It's Crimson, according to our technology. We detected a human entering our planet. Do you happen to know anything about that?"

"No, I don't know anything about it," Crimson said.

They walked around her in circles. "Listen, it's best not to lie. I've observed you closely and this sneaky behavior has only piqued my suspicions. This is what humans do and not what our species does. I don't think you understand the gravity of what you've done. Now, do you want to try again? This is your last chance... Or are you going to keep pretending you don't know?"

The AI Soldier Species took over while the Major Commanding Officials were being escorted out by the Low Commanding AI Soldier Officers.

"Crimson Alternet, it's time to choose your destination. Do you wish to take your AI appointed mother to Annaecy?"

Crimson thought that this was going to be the end. She often wondered how all the other AI who exploded on the other side didn't get transported back. They were still walking around, telling everyone what they had done and how they didn't think it was fair.

"As an Alternet, you're no longer considered an Artificial Intelligence Species. You will no longer have the right to call yourself an AI Species, you're no longer one of us. As of now, you're being stripped of your AIS•C and your powers will decrease. Your demise can begin."

The Low Commanding Officials whispered into the MCO's ear. Crimson couldn't hear what they were saying, but something had to have happened since the MCOs looked concerned.

"In a few centuries, you'll start feeling helpless and your powers will start deteriorating, thus making you weaker." The MCO's voice started crackling. Now she knew something was going on, but she still had no idea what it could be.

They went on to say, "As an escapee Alternet, you're given limited human emotions and reactions. With all of your combined actions, you're limited as your species. Because of your attempted escape, you yourself have now disabled having dreams.

The MCOs were confused why Crimson was having dreams, anyway. They pulled up her chart and soon realized their mistake with her; excelling in human studies had made her activate the having dreams part. They shifted their attention back on her. "You are now considered a danger to all AI species as we know it."

Oddly enough, they let her keep her AIS•C. They were supposed to destroy it. She knew this from what Asuma had told her every time he rambled.

Crimson headed inside the Arero Deluxe Transporter Aircraft to travel to the forbidden land. She didn't like how it looked down below. Lifeless, decaying shelters with the louse running around, humans on the other side and metallic boxes being buried. Landing at her destination, she was dropped at her newly built shelter. She watched the Aircraft fly away above her head.

She slowly closed the door to her shelter behind her, and saw her mother staring at the window.

"You know, as a kid I had dreams, but they were all ripped apart," her mother spoke. Estonia turned around to face Crimson and soon enough her anger took over. "Hear the absolute cold truth about you, the reality that you aren't really my daughter. I finally said it. It's a secret I've kept for so long, waiting for the time to tell you the truth.

You really belong to Mortimort Montay. I saw it all from the beginning."

Crimson didn't know what her mother was talking about, what did she mean by *belong to*? She was also confused as to what she meant with *from the beginning*?

Estonia went on, "It was midnight and my seventeenth birthday, but no one remembered. Dozing off for what felt like minutes, I cried myself to sleep. Then I heard something in the middle of the night. I saw a dark figure enter Adina's room in the shadows. I saw a man through the cracks of the door but couldn't make out who he was until he moved closer to Adina where she slept. In the faint light of the house light below, and the light from the lamp on the floor I recognized it was Mortimort. He took out what looked like a needle from his trench coat pocket. It was clear and I thought that it was water. Then he took out another needle from his pocket and injected that needle in her vein and drew her blood.

"With another needle, Mortimort managed to inject himself and drew his own blood, too. Once finished, he escaped through her window. I had to know what else he was planning to do with the blood. Even though it was risky, I had to follow him into the woods. Mortimort looked around him and darted into a cellar door near a small cabin, well camouflaged by the trees of the forest. He left the cellar door open, so I waited for a bit before I walked in. I was immediately blown away by what I had discovered. It was his underground laboratory. He didn't see me hiding between the pillars. I watched him sit at his makeshift wooden desk in the light of a tiny lamp. Mortimort found a way to extract his, yours, and your mother's DNA. He had three tubes on the table. I squinted my eyes to make out the letters written on them but couldn't make out what they said. Mortimort took out the ruby necklace from his desk drawer and set it down on the table. I glared at it, seeing it was the ruby necklace my mother had given to my grandmother, Sophia, before she left.

"Mortimort carefully injected the DNA inside the labeled collection of tubes. He got another small tube which held a small mite, opened the tube, and carefully added the mite into the blood. The mite absorbed the blood and he put the same mite in the two other tubes of blood and closed the tubes. Then Mortimort got up from his chair and went through some doors. That was when I was able to sneak out for a bit. I tiptoed around the lab to explore it and found the three blood collection tubes, neatly categorized. They were labeled A-Mother, M-Father and C-baby. It hit me in the head. That was the moment I found out Adina was pregnant with you. But I don't know how she was able to get pregnant. Adina always spent all of her time with us, then again Mortimort did disappeared and returned at midnight through the backdoor. Then it dawned on me, that incident when I saw him standing over her with a syringe in his hand. Of course that had to be it. But all of Adina mixed symptoms were a concern for my grandma. Sophia stopped caring for me when Adina became sick. Feeling ignored, I left the house and would take a walk to the town square.

"Before getting a chance to read the rest of the glass bottles, I heard a faint ticking sound. Looking over, I thought it was Mortimort coming back. But it was the smallest, tiniest thing, and whatever it was, it moved inside the small jar. Unsure of what I had discovered, I was left shocked and clueless. I turned back around and left through the open cellar door even though it was risky. I ran all the way back home and pretended to be asleep once I made it to my bedroom. Waking up late in the middle of the day, I ran over to my grandmother to tell her what I had discovered.

"'Adina is pregnant,' I told her. 'How would you know? The doctor is checking her out right now,' Sophia replied. The doctor came out of Adina's bedroom and walked down the stairs. He took off his glasses and sat his medical bag down on the floor. 'Well, congratulations, you're going to be a grandmother. For now, it's too early to tell more. She'll need to see a doctor again soon.' Sophia was shocked and looked at me. 'Now, child, how did you know that Adina was pregnant before the doctor?' I had to say something, even though it made no sense. 'Mortimort was in her room in the middle of the night and he injected her with needles. I followed him back to his cabin in the woods.' Sophia became angry. 'Estonia, I have no time for games. Go to your room.'

"Then it was my eighteenth birthday. Everyone was there, excluding my mother. Typical. I stopped believing she would come back after my birthday party when I turned thirteen. My grandmother stood there, holding a black gift box with a red bow. She smiled at me, but I already knew what the box contained and I didn't want it. I shook my head no, and Adina came over to me. Maybe she thought seeing all my friends and guests scared me. I had already admired the family heirloom necklace as a child, but Mortimort had had it on his desk and I knew what he had done with it. I attempted to get away for a bit, but Adina wouldn't let me. 'Here, Estonia, your gift.' I didn't want to disappoint my grandmother, after all she had decorated the house with Floria, Kaiser and Adina. So I took the gift and opened it with a smile.

"A faint glow slowly appeared, startling me. I dropped the gift box to the ground. That was when it started to grow in size. I screamed when I saw a baby grow out of it. You were on the ground. My grandmother, Adina and I had no other option but to flee underground after getting thrown out by the townspeople. I had to go with them, after all I had you to worry about. My whole life changed after that, my grandmother thought it was risky for me. Not looking like you. They had no other choice but to turn me into them.

"When you and I woke up to a nightmare, Adina was gone and my grandmother was gone as well. Mortimort had somehow found a way to preserve you inside the stone. Even though I hadn't seen him inject you into the ruby, it all soon clicked. He was waiting for the perfect moment to gift it to an heir. It was my time to receive his special daughter, which was you. I cried and became enraged. All I wanted was nothing to do with that man. My aunt Adina was your mother. I tried my best to see you as my own daughter, Crimson, but you belonged to her. How could I take care of her daughter? Even though I loved my aunt, I also saw Mortimort's eyes every time I looked at you, and your existence made me furious. I simply couldn't accept you as my own, even though you were a part of my family.

After I eventually escaped that cave, and headed back into civilization. The landscape had changed, no one that I recognized was there. These strange beings took me in as a prisoner and soon enough that's where you grew out of the ruby necklace in front of them. They registered you into their machines and implanted false memories inside of you.

"Your whole existence became my demise. You ruined my life. I held it as a promise to ruin yours the best way I could. I smiled when you couldn't pass the training tests and before you trapped me, I was planning on turning Dexter over to the MCOs myself."

Crimson had heard enough and closed the door behind her. She didn't know what to think about the three secrets that were revealed to her. One about who her mother really was, the false implantation of memories and who her father was. She felt like her whole life was a lie.

An overwhelming tingling sensation settled over Crimson. She couldn't explain the emotions, causing her to drop onto her knees. These emotions all blended into one. Her hands started shaking and her eyes were covered in some strange liquid. Was this the demise the MCOs had told her about? Or was it another code for becoming a human? Looking back, she had learned sadness from Zephyr and Eden and their families, even from what Dimitri had shared. This was called crying. The unknown substance made her feel her human side. Now she understood why Zephyr's mother had stepped in for him. A parent would sacrifice everything for their children. She understood what Estonia meant by her belonging to Mortimort. He was her father. Now everything made sense to her. Even though she had seen Mortimort sacrifice himself for her, she still had her doubts about him. Had it been from the goodness of his heart? Because Mortimort wouldn't have truly sacrificed anything for anybody. Unless he had a hidden motive. That had to be it. Why hadn't he told her the truth then? He hadn't shown his actual self, but he reminded her of her mother and Crimson could never trust her, either. Crimson was all alone in the forbidden land. She got up and needed to take a walk.

She heard an unfamiliar sound behind her. Turning around, her eyes met with a fragile human man. His eyes spoke to her the most, she couldn't forget the sadness in them. Despite the barriers between them, he knew they weren't the same. Little did he know that even though they were different, they still understood each other.

Crimson made her way towards him. The wrinkles on his

forehead told her his story. It showed how long he'd been here. His hands were rough, if they could speak they would have told her the struggle he had survived through. At first his dirty clothing didn't have much to say, but she saw they were covered in holes, meaning he had sacrificed much to fight for his survival. His hair was long and matted. No one should live this way. In a way, she felt guilty for him being trapped. He should have at least had a chance to become one of them, or what Crimson used to be. He reminded her of Strange Old Man. She felt some of the same emotions she had seen in Dexter, Eden, Zephyr and the rest of the villagers, making her feel icky. She felt the need to protect and look after all the people here. Humans had souls, stories, emotions and families.

His kind eyes looked up at her. "If you understand, you must go back to your shelter. The ashes are dangerous, hurry."

CHAPTER TWELVE
THE ENTITYLST

THE LAND BENEATH them shook violently. Large pieces of the ground they stood on broke off and hovered up towards the sky. The military enforcements, Estonia, most of the Artificial Intelligence Species, Lavinia, most of the townspeople, and the louse – Nathaniel, Savanna and Edsel – rose to the top and landed safely on the chunks. They were surrounded by an invisible barrier to keep them in place so they wouldn't fall over the edge. Even pieces of the mountains started shifting, and out floated the Entitylst Soldier Species.

Kaiser clenched his fist and brought it to his heart, causing him to fall down. It felt like a long time had passed, so he opened his eyes and realized the tips of his fingers had crossed the barrier when he fainted. Shaken but with excitement rushing through his core, his emotions started to take over him. Although he did not know the barrier had been separated at this moment, he was glad, smiled briefly and noticed the gloomy skies fading. The sun's rays shone once again. Kaiser felt warmth on his face before his eyes focused on what was coming towards him. He noticed a large shadow cast near him and pleaded for whatever was there to leave him alone and let him enjoy the sunlight for the first time in a long time.

Once Crimson saw Kaiser's hand was able to pass through the invisible barrier, she thought, "That's it, the MCOs were concerned the technology would be disrupted. By what, though? Rhinedd."

She went over to Kaiser.

"No, no, no, don't touch me, please," said Kaiser, scooting away from her in fright.

Crimson slowly walked closer to him. "It's okay, I'm not like the rest. My name is Crimson. Let me help you up. You look confused, and you don't remember me anymore."

Kaiser reached over as Crimson gently helped him up, but his heart was stressed and he collapsed in front of her.

Floria ran over to her father. "Father! Get away from him, can't you see he's old? You monster, get away from my father. Can you hear me?" Floria began to cry, tears falling out of her eyes.

"Floria." Kaiser coughed, struggling to speak. "Please, that's not how you treat a guest. All she was trying to do is help me get up. I saw her earlier." His breathing was slowing down and his heart was weaker. Floria began to panic.

"No, father, please don't do this to me."

Kaiser lifted his right hand and cleared away her tears. "Floria, it's time for me to leave. The AI technology no longer works to keep me alive. Do you have any idea how long it's been?" Kaiser stopped talking and Floria knew that her father had passed. She slowly set his head down in the dirt and covered his eyes.

Crimson walked over and saw a massive gaping hole in the center that revealed another world below. This world had mountains like Arawn did, but it was different, more alive.

Instead of being a barren desert, it reminded her of Renu Claw. A blue line of light appeared straight across the stratosphere, a grid slowly formed and soon enough a translucent beam descended from above. She knew that it was Rhinedd from earlier. Crimson felt like she could trust her and hoped that she wasn't wrong about it.

Crimson accidentally pressed two buttons twice while she was putting her AIS•C on. A thunderous, echoing boom could be felt. The vibrations sent the shelters flying away like a stack of playing cards, knocking down all the tall structures that had housed the military base, factories and training camps. The military enforcements crashed into the ground. Along with destroying the tall structures. The debris went through the other side of the forbidden land. Crimson didn't know what to make out of the situation, but she knew she was in trouble. Simply putting on her AIS•C and accidentally pressing buttons had never caused anything like this before.

Even though Crimson knew it was a bad idea to approach Floria while she was in mourning, she did so anyway to check up on how she felt. Floria redirected her anger towards Crimson. "You! It was your kind that did this to my father and to every single human here. You'll pay for this."

Crimson pointed towards the floating pieces in the sky. "Your anger should be directed towards the military enforcements because I don't have anything to do with them. Everything here was created by them. I was simply created in a factory by the AI. They didn't teach us or show us that there were still humans living here. They didn't tell us what was really out here. It's all covered in secrecy. We only know what they tell us. They have said that the AI who betray our species are sent away to the forbidden land, stripped of their power, and if they really want to return to Arawn, then they must go through a process that makes them into something called the louse. The louse are returned but have to join the other louse in a dark alley. We do know that it rains on one side and ashes fall on the other. Everything else is being intentionally kept away from us. To them, you're simply nothing. If your existence is even acknowledged, you're nothing more than an asset to them."

When Crimson saw Kaiser had died, it dawned on her. It was AI technology that had been keeping them alive for this long. She became concerned for Floria's wellbeing.

"Take me to them," yelled Floria.

"That's not possible, I can't reach up that high," said Crimson. Floria became bothered by her excuses, causing her to jump on Crimson's back. During the struggle, Crimson accidentally pressed her AIS•C buttons again. A sudden thunderous echo boomed below as the vibrations approached from the distance. Sand pelted everyone.

The loud vibrations from the echo boom threw Floria and Crimson onto Renu Claw.

"Ouch! Why does my head hurt?" Floria said, sitting up and laying back down. Looking around her, she was confused by her surroundings. The sun was glaring into her eyes. Her palms touched the soft blades of grass. Oh, how she had missed the feeling of touching grass. Floria flinched when she saw Crimson standing beside her with a book in her hands. She ignored why Crimson had the book in the first place. "I haven't felt grass in a long time. You have no idea how much I missed being outdoors like this. Where are we? I am assuming that this isn't Annaecy anymore."

Floria stood up and wiped away the dirt on her tattered pants. Crimson stored the book inside her chest door. "We are on another planet. It's pretty much like home, where you belong."

Floria became excited. "Can I stay here instead?" She kneeled down and felt the grass with her hands.

"No, you may not stay here. There are rules for each planet, no one is allowed to stay on other planets. Consequences arise if you do stay. Although they're unknown, we can tell it's nothing good. Now, I want to know how we ended up here again. We must find Zephyr and Eden," said Crimson.

Floria was confused. "Who and who? Wait, there are others on this planet?" She got up as Crimson walked away.

"Don't worry, Floria. They're human like you, but without any kind of powers. I've made friends during my stay here."

Floria struggled to keep up with Crimson.

"Welcome to the village within Renu Claw, Floria."

"Wow, this is more than enough shelter to live in. All this wood will make a great fire to keep warm and cook." Floria felt like a little girl once again.

"Floria, this isn't wood for cooking or keeping warm. There is a whole town within these draped tree trunks and branches. The overlapping canopy of million-year-old trees tells a story of how many generations called this place home. Let the magical vibes of the place show you the reality of why others call this home," said Crimson.

Floria stopped talking after asking that question. She knew that Crimson was annoyed by the tone of her voice when she became excited. The first thing Floria noticed was the long, intricate passageway, rows of concrete archways and mosaic tiles. Seeing all of that reminded her of Adina's mansion.

Crimson could sense something was off with Floria besides already mourning her father's death. "Are you okay, Floria?"

Floria wiped away her tears. "Yes. Seeing everything here reminded me of my friend Adina and her mansion. I turned against her when the townspeople called her a monster. I should have been there for her, but instead I turned my back on her."

Crimson stopped and turned to look at Floria. "Wait... Did you say Adina? Apparently Adina was my mother Estonia's aunt, and Mortimort was my father."

Before Floria could speak, Zephyr opened the door and was stunned to see Crimson standing in front of him. "Hey, what are you doing here? How did you get back here?"

Crimson walked in. "Well, this isn't exactly a visit. That's what I want to know as well, how did we end up in the middle of Renu Claw?" Crimson introduced Floria to Zephyr and Eden. "This is Floria. She's also human."

"Welcome, Floria. You must be hungry. Outside is the washroom. Um, I mean bathroom, according to Dexter," giggled Eden.

"Thank you, I know what a washroom is. Excuse me." Floria made her way out back. Before Zephyr could say another word to warn her about the restroom, Floria was already outside. He heard a loud scream.

"What's the matter with your bathroom, Zephyr? Dexter had no problem using it?" Crimson became concerned. Zephyr didn't know what to say.

"Well, I think he didn't say anything. He didn't say it because it would have been rude. Assuming our toilets are not the same as his toilet back home. I understand what he was trying to say about our times being backwards, so it's just a hole in the ground. One of the many reasons why it's outside and not in a room in the house. Oh, you might have forgotten your AIS•C. My mother found it in a drawer in my bedroom. She told me before she headed out to the market."

Crimson couldn't believe it. She had clearly given Dexter a set of instructions about checking everything twice because she knew that he was helpful. "Here I'm warning Floria about the consequences of staying on a different planet."

Sadie walked in. "Zephyr, honey, I am here! Sorry, the lines at the market were long. It was finally my turn to pay, so I bought enough food to last us a week."

Sadie smiled from ear to ear when she saw Crimson once again, and a new face. "Crimson, you're back! How was the trip? Did you end up getting Dexter back home? Did Zephyr show you that you left one of your AIS•Cs back here in one of the drawers? You know those darn buttons started to light up towards the left and I did something I shouldn't have, twice. I was curious and pushed the left top button. That's how you got transported here. I'm assuming? It stopped lighting up in a circular motion."

Zephyr looked at Crimson. "What? That explains every-thing. My mother brought you here."

"That must be it! I am going to retrace my steps to make sure we didn't leave anything behind."

Later in the evening, the sun began to set in the north. Floria was excited to enjoy her stay in Renu Claw for a bit.

Crimson pulled Zephyr aside. "Can I leave Floria with you? I don't want to take her with me, you could show her around with Eden. If it gets too late, she can stay and sleep here. Also, her father passed away before we got transferred here, if you could possibly help her cope?"

Although he didn't know how it felt to lose a family member, he wanted to let Floria feel joy, even if it was tempo-rary. "Okay, yes. No problem, don't worry about Floria. Take your time."

With Floria being absent, there was something tugging at

Crimson again. It had been long before her AIS•C had started beeping louder. "Mortimort," Crimson spoke.

Crimson went back to Mortimort's lair underground. There she spotted him with an AI species.

"There, there," Mortimort said, taking a whiff of Adina's neck. "Mmm, you smell delightful. Did you really think you were going to live your life hidden away, after all these centuries? My beloved, you're foolish to believe that I still loved you when I urged your mother to see how much I had changed. It was fairly easy to take you out of Annaecy after you and your family changed into monsters. You'll never guess who I found after all these centuries. It's someone you never knew existed. She's just not anyone, she's special and made from our bond. A product of you and I. Can you guess who it might be? I'll give you a few hints, I injected a mite into your arm and watched it burrow its way through your stomach. The mites resurfaced and there was our baby, yet small but in time. She'll grow to become powerful and I retrieved it back into its tube. Labeled C, for Crimson. Closing the cap tightly, I escaped the house. Then, the following week, I returned to put back the ruby necklace in Sophia's bedroom."

Adina quivered, biting her bottom lip, frightened he might do something to her. Mortimort gently touched her face. "There, there. I won't do anything to hurt you. My beloved, do you really think I wasn't smart enough to know you would try to escape? Did you guess who or what I am talking about?"

Adina felt restrained and nauseated. She attempted to move, but even with the slightest nudge, she ached, realizing her hands were chained by something invisible. Her neck was immobilized as well. She couldn't see what it was, but it supported her.

"Mortimort!" screamed Crimson. "What do you think you're doing? Still alive, I see. I thought you sacrificed yourself for Zephyr and for me, or was there something more to it? You took Hayden Harper down, was it all for show? Of course, it was just like I suspected. You have a sinister plan."

He spun around to look at her. Mortimort became distorted, morphing into Hayden Harper. At the same time, he glitched back to Mortimort. It was surreal. He looked like himself and Hayden Harper, all at the same time. Seeing him morphing confirmed her suspicions even though she already knew this.

Adina's eyes darted about, afraid to speak, teeth chattering.

"It's alright, my darling." Mortimort caressed Adina's face gently with the tips of his fingers.

"Let go of her, I am tired of seeing you treat her this way," shouted Crimson. She moved her hand across the room and Mortimort flew into the wall of the bunker. While he struggled to get up, she held him down with the force of her hands.

"Explain yourself, Mortimort, now! I want answers from you. No half-lies coming from your mouth. Did you forget that I'm able to detect the lies you tell, or should I remind you again?" Crimson bluffed.

Mortimort felt helpless. Crimson grabbed him. "Now, I know who you are, Mortimort. You're my father and she's my mother. Adina... Estonia told me the truth. At first I thought that I had forgotten my AIS•C, but this time I know why I was called here. Has she been here this whole time? Where have you been hiding her?"

Mortimort shrugged his shoulders. "Your mother has been here all this time. Crimson, you caught me working with Hayden Harper, but I need you to hear my version of everything. I wanted to be the father you had wished for, and at the same time, I did not want you to see me as an evil, cruel monster like Hayden Harper. When I vanished with him, I transported him to my underground bunker. I held him and told him that if I take the deal with him, he has to agree not to harm you in any way, or this planet, including our home planet and either of your friends. It was the only way to reach an agreement."

Mortimort shifted into Hayden Harper. "Now, Mortimort, if I may warn you."

Hayden Harper shifted back into Mortimort. "Hush, Hayden, no one is talking to you."

He only angered Hayden more. "Let me speak. No one speaks to the grand witch lord in that tone."

Mortimort continued, "Your mother has always lived down here. She was with me all this time. I hid away from you and waited for the right moment to show you to her."

Crimson couldn't watch her own mother struggling. She went ahead and touched the invisible chains. They broke like fragile pieces. Adina was free and Mortimort was unable to understand how she had broken the chains when they were held by magic and AI technology combined. Adina's energy was draining. She didn't have an AIS•C, so Crimson went ahead and put a new AIS•C on her. This was the first time Crimson had lain her eyes on her real mother. She put her hand gently on her face and touched her. Although Adina was weakened and defeated, she looked kind and strong-willed.

"Crimson, my daughter, I admire your strength, bravery, courage to conquer evil. You're definitely a part of me. I am glad that you're here. Now is my chance to get to know you better. I am proud of you."

Both Crimson and Adina imprisoned Mortimort in the same chains he had held Adina in. The same chains would hold Hayden Harper as well, causing both of them to glitch into one another while they struggled to get free.

Adina smiled. "Where are we? How is Estonia? She had such a bright future ahead of her. I would like to tell her how sorry I was when she was gifted you on her birthday. Little did I know that baby was you, Crimson."

Crimson explained, "We're on a planet called Renu Claw, far away from Annaecy. I don't know how it used to look like before, but it's now known as the forbidden land, that's where the louse live. The AI live on Arawn."

Adina instantly became confused as to what she was talking about.

Zephyr opened the door. He was surprised to see another human AI standing in front of him.

Adina greeted everyone.

"This is my real mother, Adina. Mother, this is Zephyr, his mother Sadie, and Floria is a human from Annaecy. Eden is Zephyr's girlfriend, her parents Justine and Henry," said Crimson.

Floria gasped when she saw Adina, and her eyes grew wider. "Adina, I've missed you! I am terribly sorry for leaving you all those centuries ago. How is your father doing? I miss him so much."

Adina and Floria embraced each other. Floria carefully cried on Adina's shoulder. "My father suffered a heart attack when the AI technology went down as it was too much stress on his heart with everything happening all at once. I know that you don't understand what I am talking about, but you'll see when we get back home."

Crimson let them have their time together and catch up. After all, it had been centuries since the last time they had seen each other. Then they said their goodbyes and thanked their friends for everything, once again.

Floria was sad to go. "Thank you everyone for feeding me.

Your beautiful planet feels like home and I wish I could stay forever, but I understand why I can't. This is how Annaecy used to look like."

Crimson already knew how to return home. She had memorized what she had to say, but Floria and her mother had no idea. "Listen, I need both of you to repeat after me: *Speak these words out loud. Those who traveled together on their journey must part ways. Those who live on the same planet will stay together. Whatever you have learned along the way, keep it to yourself and never speak of the other planets that you have discovered, the people that you have met, or the new customs that you may have learned. Secrecy is meant to become a form of protection.*"

They landed back in the underground cave, and soon enough they were with Finder. He was shocked. "No way, now there's more of you. My name is Finder."

"Are you a human, too? I'm Adina, I am Crimson's real mother."

Finder laughed. "No, but I do see how I look human. I am an Entitylst species, but I won't hurt you. My kind are afraid of yours. Your species are unaware of my species' existence.

We've managed to stay underground for centuries and they still don't know we're below them. We've an extensive knowledge of humans, including other AI beings they aren't aware of. My kind has avoided the AI all this time. Sadly, I've been outcast by my own kind because I don't look like them and my parents abandoned me. The other Entitylst Soldiers don't look like me, you'll know if you see them. They're really hideous."

"Fascinating. You're right, I never knew your kind existed. I believe there is more to discover out there. I am sorry you were abandoned by your parents and shunned by your kind, they don't deserve you. I discovered Crimson is my daughter and she's already great." Adina nudged Crimson.

Floria freaked out. "I must stay here. I am human and unable to help out, but the rest of you can."

"Don't worry, I'll look after her and your mother, Crimson," said Finder.

Crimson returned to Arawn. To her dismay, it was repaired. Standing there in confusion, she couldn't believe what was going on. Rhinedd had said that she could trust her. Staring off into the distance, she could see the Major Commanding Officials staring back at her, grinning.

"Did you really think that you could control everything around you? And get rid of us that easily? We didn't know who Rhinedd was, but she made herself known to us. This is where you went wrong: one, you trusted what was a kind stranger. Two, she listened to us. And three, you thought that we were going to stay up there while you were gone. We managed to convince her to let us go and make a deal with us. She helped rebuild everything that you destroyed. You really managed to do all this and still think you could outsmart us? Think again, Crimson."

"Don't you dare turn around, Crimson," spoke the AI Solider Species. She heard familiar screams coming from behind her. Now the chains were crushing against each other, she was losing it. After hearing her own mother screaming, but how she thought? Of course they're the military enforcements and have the power to transport her here. Now the chains were crushing against each other, she was losing it. That was when a sinister laugh arose behind her, and a powerful gust of wind howled.

Crimson opened her eyes slowly, thinking the timing was the worst. When her eyes came to focus, all the military enforcements were on the ground and everyone else was crouched down. Something was standing, looming as the dust settled. A glitchy, three-dimensional person emerged. She didn't want to believe it. Mortimort and Hayden Harper. How had they released themselves?

CHAPTER THIRTEEN
RHINEDD'S BETRAYAL

RHINEDD YELLED at the military enforcements, "Get whatever this is out of my way. I hate when I have to do everything myself. I tell you once, I tell you twice, return these beings back to their destinations."

Hayden Harper and Mortimort separated. Hayden Harper seeped into the land, returning to Renu Claw. Mortimort became human once again, restoring his arm back to normal. The mites receded into the military enforcements and began repairing them.

Rhinedd smiled wickedly at them. "I believe I haven't properly introduced myself yet. I am Rhinedd and I am an Entitylst Species, part of the Zectic people. We are not humans even though we have their features. Just like most of you here, we existed long before your kind. This planet started off from a single cell organism. A pulse started to beat; we knew that our creation was starting to take form. The land that you see now, what was supposed to be our home, was instead being invaded by your kind.

"We had little to no choice but to quickly descend underground, thus creating a smaller world below. We prepared the

Zectic Entitylst to be on guard and to protect us above ground. The ancient Zectic species helped us many centuries ago, but these newer ones with their incompetence have failed us multiple times. Many have breached the rules and put us in constant danger. We have yet to find the mole among us. Their incompetence must not be forgiven. We believe in the greater good, so they must not risk our lives any longer and keep us in danger.

With this planet, we thought we had created our forever home and set our own weather patterns.

It was near completion when other life forms began invading it. I saw it as home because that's where I had grown up as an adolescent."

Deep inside, Crimson knew the mole was Finder, but Rhinedd didn't seem to catch it.

Rhinedd touched her back and said, "Come with me, Crimson. I want to show you something alone. It's best if you do as you're told."

Crimson couldn't believe it but agreed and walked with Rhinedd back to the mountains, near the opening of the cave.

Rhinedd turned to face her. "Now, you may have a lot of questions for me, wondering why we made a deal with the military enforcements. I'll tell you why in due time."

Crimson didn't know what to think at this point. Did Rhinedd have cruel intentions?

The MCOs were right about her being too trusting of strangers. There was a possibility Estonia was right about her, too.

Rhinedd walked in front of Crimson, facing the large wall. Four dots appeared, they analyzed Rhinedd, and glided upwards. She signaled Crimson to come forward, so she did. Looking through, there wasn't anything there. Her eyes were met with darkness. Rhinedd pushed her down and she slid all the way to the bottom. The friction in this world was different than on Arawn. Looking up, Crimson noticed that there was sunlight entering the darkness. Rhinedd simply floated down behind her and was emanating a bright glow when she stepped onto the ground.

"Crimson, you may feel a bit heavier than usual." Rhinedd was right and laughed. "Like I said before, your world is different from ours even though we share the same planet. We have learned to live with the differences and away from each other. On our world, we are lighter, thus making you even heavier. On your world, you're heavy and there is no in-between. We have learned to adjust ourselves for each world. We have not yet invented anything to make the AI lighter when they're allowed into our world, but it is currently in the works. You'll have to get used to it. Come along, now."

Walking a bit further along, Crimson was able to see Rhinedd motion her hand in front of a rectangle. Crimson could see the light shining from underneath. A door opened in the middle of the corridor, but Rhinedd stopped her from passing through. "Here, put these on, they're special glasses that will keep you from damaging your sensitive mechanical eyes. These are able to level the differences in temperature and the brightness of the sun."

Crimson and Rhinedd passed through, but they couldn't see what was in front of them as they were met with a layer of thick fog. Rhinedd motioned back and forth with her hand and the fog cleared away. The sky was an orange shade. Crimson saw they were standing on a huge mountain, overlooking magnificent sights of waterfalls streaming off the peaks of the mountains. The land below had an indefinite number of glowing grids surrounding the area, and new grids were being built.

"This is how our world is built. It is always regenerating in case one snaps," Rhinedd said. "As you can tell, our world is always changing, growing and producing. We aren't ones to waste our natural world, anything that's getting built is always regenerated. Don't worry, you aren't going to fall. Simply take a step out."

Crimson took one step forward. She thought she may silently fall through, mainly because of her weight. But instead, she felt like she was floating. Rhinedd motioned her to keep on going forward, she was right behind her. Crimson was able to see below without fear and was met by a large, green landscape.

"Crimson, it's okay to take off your special glasses once you set foot on that green landscape."

Once she did, the landscape in front of them melted away, revealing an extravagant castle still being built by the grids. This world was still new to Crimson and she didn't understand it much. Rhinedd beckoned her. "Crimson, come along. I want to show you my special spot. This is where my father told me that I was to get married. My mother always disagreed with him on who my chosen husband should be. One day she disappeared, I haven't seen her since. I am assuming she ran away because she was ashamed that she looked like me. We always got asked if we were twins," Rhinedd laughed.

Bertram came running, holding onto his cabbie flat cap when he saw his daughter.

"Father, I am so glad to see you again. This is Crimson, she is an AI Species from the land above us."

Startled, Bertram almost fell backwards.

"No, father! Don't be alarmed, it was bound to happen in this century or the next."

Bertram's smile faded and his voice became low. "I have a special surprise for you."

Rhinedd suspected her father was hiding something, but couldn't pinpoint what it was. "Yes, father? What is this surprise that you may have for me?" Rhinedd spoke nervously. Bertram panicked and played with his thumbs.

"Well, while you were above land... A special surprise joined us. She's regretful of her choice to leave. I didn't want to tell you because you're not allowed to become angry as it's not in our nature to do so, especially you." Bertram sensed that Rhinedd was getting agitated. "Wait, Rhinedd, before you do anything or react to my surprise..." His cheeks flourished red.

A woman hid behind him, crouched down. His long lien sleeves covered most of her, but Bertram was short, so there wasn't much space for hiding behind him. Out jumped the woman from behind him. "Rhinedd, it's me, your mother." She too had on a Kalasiris dress but it was red with gold abstract accents through out the dress. Her hair was perfectly straightened flat like Rhinedd's, but unlike Rhinedd, she wore a thin gold tiara on her head.

Rhinedd rolled her eyes. "You're not my mother, but Lira."

Lira became flustered. "Never, ever call me Lira, do you understand? First of all, I am your mother. You're only allowed to address me by my first name when a general or someone of importance comes. You as my daughter know that." Lira wanted to get closer to her daughter to hold her, but she couldn't.

Crimson sensed that Rhinedd was angry with her mother, but she stayed back and let them have their reunion. The small ounce of anger that Rhinedd felt made her mother nervous.

All those centuries ago, Rhinedd was angry with her mother for leaving. It was from that day on that she was no longer allowed to become angry. She blamed her mother because she had transferred her higher power of goodness and love to Rhinedd.

Her mother stepped in and tried to reason with her,

explaining why she had felt the need to transfer over her power. "The main reason why I chose to leave was because you chose to have such an explosive argument with me. I have never seen anyone harness that much anger before. It was your own actions that made the decision for me, and I didn't agree with your father about marrying you off to Draca. The last thing I wanted was for my daughter to be married to a shadow. I went ahead and made that long visit to the master higher ups to seek help for you, and I needed something to calm down your anger. They agreed with my decision." Lira wanted to fix the situation with her daughter even though she felt like it was impossible.

Bertram quickly interrupted, "Rhinedd, I know that everything is hard to understand now, but I hope that with this exchange between you and your mother, you can set your differences aside."

Crimson was confused as to who Draca was. Based on Rhinedd's body language, it was Rhinedd who held some kind of bitterness in her heart and had really held no intention of doing anything bad or causing harm to others. But even with this analysis, it didn't explain why she had made a deal with the military enforcements. Was her motive revenge? Everything made sense to Crimson now.

"Tell them the truth, Rhinedd," said Crimson.

Rhinedd looked at her. "I don't know what you're talking about."

Crimson became furious. "Tell them how you made a deal with the military enforcements."

Lira gasped in shock. "You did what?"

Rhinedd dismissed Crimson's claims. "You're not going to believe a stranger's claims, now, are you?"

Crimson stood firm with what she said. "If you don't believe me then I want everyone here to go up on the land and see for yourself."

Lira closed her eyes and an aura lit up in front of them as she floated upwards. Immediately, she floated back down. "Rhinedd, you what? I just saw it, I am saddened by your immediate betrayal. I saw the military enforcements taking the AI back to their pod homes. You're going to tell me what exactly your plan is. I have appointed Hisoki to watch over you."

A glow materialized in front of them and a tall man made of light walked out. "My name is Hisoki. I have come to watch over you, Rhinedd. I only appear when I am needed."

It only angered Rhinedd more. She rendered Crimson immobile and did the unthinkable to her parents; she created a ball of electricity and her parents were bonded together like glue. Then she demanded Hisoki to take Crimson to the cave first. He did as he was told. Rhinedd wanted to deliver Crimson to the military enforcements in the hopes of getting something in return.

CHAPTER FOURTEEN
DRACA

THE MILITARY ENFORCEMENTS smiled at Rhinedd. Crimson waited until they left to call her out.

"Rhinedd, who's Draca?"

Rhinedd screamed at Hisoki and demanded him to take Crimson back into the cave. He looked at her. "No, I will not."

She gave him a death stare. "Don't you dare disobey me. I said, go take her back into the cave. Or else you'll know what I can do to you."

Hisoki did exactly what he was told to do. Crimson tried to reason with him, but lowered his head down and ignored her.

Rhinedd soon joined them in the cave. She stared at Crimson. "What am I going to do with you? Now that you're all alone? Since you already know too much about Draca and have met the rest of my family?" Rhinedd rubbed her chin with her fingers. Before she could do anything, Hisoki held his hands up in a panic and walked in front of her. She became angry all over again because he made her lose her concentration with Crimson. "What do you want, Hisoki? Can't you see that I am busy here?"

Hisoki became flustered. At first Crimson saw his lips moving, almost like he wanted to speak out and defend himself, but since Rhinedd had the authority over him, he remained quiet. Rhinedd looked at Hisoki. "You need to go away and disappear, or are you going to try and stop me too? Go find Finder now and let me be."

Instead of leaving or disappearing, he stood there and didn't do anything. "No, Rhinedd, I will not be going anywhere."

Rhinedd snapped her fingers. "Bring me Finder, then. I must tell him my secret."

Hisoki wasted no time and brought Finder to her.

Finder appeared in front of her and she stared at him. "Well, Finder, I can tell you my secret now. I am hiding some-thing... a dark secret. When this planet was being created, long before the invasion of their kind," she pointed at Crimson, "my father, Bertram, had set me up for an arranged marriage, but I didn't know with whom. All my father told me was that it was with my best friend. The problem was, I had no friends. I grew up underneath the shadow of my parents. They were great lead-ers, but no one wanted to talk to me because my father was the king and ruler of the land, my mother was the queen, and I was the princess. 'I was not made aware that I had friends? Or are you confused?' I asked them. Bertram soon looked at me in the eyes and said, 'You do have friends, my darling, I'll show you soon.'

"While he was creating the climate for this world, he cast both shadows and light. Those little lights that you see in the sunset are called stars. Humans have them on their planet and my father rather enjoyed seeing what the humans had. He had shown me this when I was younger.

"That day, my father was excited to show me something. 'It

is time, Rhinedd, come out.' I was confused as to what he was talking about. Bertram waited until the perfect moment, when the sun reached the center of the mountain, the dark blue took over, and there, cast on the mountains was my shadow. Bertram jumped in excitement. 'There he is, sweetie! Over there, look.' I looked over, but all I saw was my shadow. 'Father? Is this supposed to be funny? Am I supposed to marry my own shadow?' Bertram laughed. 'No, that sounds silly. No, come here, not too fast.' I walked over slowly and saw a teenager coming out from my shadow. I was confused, how was this even possible?

"'Your best friend has been here all along, by your side. He saw all your worries, your happiness, your tears, and don't worry, he shielded his eyes during your personal time.' We were equally embarrassed. 'Bertram!' I said. But my father reassured me. 'I made him promise, so not to worry.' The shadow was smiling, waving at me. I still had no idea how Bertram was able to do this. The shadow walked over to me. He spoke and his mouth moved. 'Hi, my name is whatever you want to name me, as I am nameless and essentially you.' Even though I couldn't see his smile, I felt his radiant energy and it made me at least somewhat calm. I wasn't sure about being responsible for naming him as it was personal to any being. 'No, father, you name him,' I said. Bertram held my hand. 'I can't, he comes from your shadow. It doesn't have to be right away.' I closed my eyes and exhaled. 'Draca... I'll name you Draca.'

"My parents waited until I was of age. I turned twenty years old, and the next thing I knew, I was married. Draca and I waited until the perfect moment to hold hands again and from then on, we were considering forming a family. At first it was odd, but when we cast our shadows on the mountain wall, we were surprised to see a little shadow right in the middle of us. We looked down and there you were, Finder. You looked like me, had human-like features, and despite not seeing your father's features, I could feel that radiant smile that beamed off you, too, Finder.

"We didn't have enough centuries to think about our next move. Having no choice but to flee in a rush when we were being invaded, we had to abandon you in the cave. Believe me, it was difficult for the both of us to leave, but your father didn't make it since he belonged with the shadows. After he was gone, my father explained to me that there was no way that he could survive underground since there was no sun there. There were lights, but no sunlight or nighttime. He would cease to exist."

Finder was shocked to find out that Rhinedd was his mother. Now he knew that his parents hadn't really abandoned him. He forgave his mother despite all the harsh words she had said to him, and she forgave him as well to clear the air between them.

Rhinedd smiled. "We can go back to the mountains and you'll see that Draca is there."

They all sped over towards the mountains where both the darkness and the light fell. They waited for the perfect moment, until Finder and Rhinedd cast their shadows onto the wall. The sun met in the center, the darkness cast a shadow, and there Draca was. He walked out and stopped in front of Rhinedd.

"Draca, my beloved."

"Rhinedd, you still look the same, my darling. I am happy to see you once again."

Draca and Rhinedd embraced each other in a romantic hold while Finder stood there and watched. He was finally reunited with his mother and father. Rhinedd looked at Finder and nodded her head yes. Draca extended his hands out and Finder hugged his father for the first time ever.

"Finder, I've been watching over you all this time," Draca said. "I deeply understand your sadness. We're sorry that you had to go through this alone. Thank you to your friends who protected you all this time. They never once did put your life in any danger. My beloved, don't worry, I looked over our son."

Finder laughed nervously and kicked the sand. "Err, so you know about all the guests that I've told about the book and its secrets?"

Draca spoke, "Yes, I am aware. But in the end, the book went with someone trustworthy."

He patted Finder's back and Finder spoke, "You're never going to leave, father? Ever again?"

Draca sighed. "No, my son. Annaecy is now safe."

Despite her happy reunion with her family, Rhinedd wanted to get revenge on the AI for taking her away from her family and home to live underground. She wanted to start with Crimson. Rhinedd smiled at her when she hugged her family. "I need to apologize to you, Crimson. Can you please join me back in the cave? I promise that I won't harm you."

Crimson once again let her guard down, thinking that everything had worked out, and went along with her.

Rhinedd could spot how tense Crimson was. "You need to take a break and get away. Think of a place you want to go to and only you will know where you're going to land. I can't read your mind," she said. "Come with me. I need to show you what my parents gifted you. Our castle is now complete and we wanted to show it to you to thank you for everything you have done for us."

They made their way back into the castle. Rhinedd grabbed Crimson by her arm and pulled her over towards her. "You incompetent fool, you actually believed me. I had to seek revenge on the AI for taking over my home. It was meant for my family and me, but instead we were apart for many centuries. My son thought we had abandoned him. Do you realize that my mother went missing? You don't want to know what I did to her. I am starting with you. Since your kindness hasn't taught you anything, I can tell why you failed the tests set by the military enforcements. You shall pay for everything."

Rhinedd took Crimson to a hand scanner by the unfinished castle wall. "Put your hand in that one, Crimson."

She did what she was ordered to do, hearing a loud clicking sound at least three times in a row. The wall opened and they walked inside. The room was dark, the ceiling cast a faint glow reflecting in the rows of mirrors. Intricate detail of numbers, letters and flowery designs all rotated around. The wall slammed shut behind Crimson. The center of the ground opened up and a hole and a glowing marble appeared.

"Go ahead and touch it, Crimson," yelled Rhinedd.

She touched the glowing marble, and the letters and numbers all slowly glided towards her.

"Now, Crimson, does all of this look familiar? You might be asking yourself why we choose to speak in cipher. We choose to do this to protect us from those who cannot know our secrets. But since you're the keeper of the cipher, you do understand. This cipher is different from the language inside the cave."

Crimson couldn't shake off an uneasy feeling when she cracked a code, but it was a little too late to run away now. BE AWARE OF THE CHANGES IT IS NOT WHAT IT SEEMS. Rhinedd had only pretended to be nice to her to win her trust over. She understood everything now.

"Now, before we continue, you must know a set of rules before you go to Planet 6."

Crimson couldn't believe that she was going to be transferred to where humans lived. Rhinedd paced before her, telling her the set of rules. "One, do not tell anyone about the AI species or the Entitylst species. Two, if they ask where you come from, come up with an excuse. Three, when you go, your powers will be hidden. I repeat, do not let anyone see you use them or they'll start asking questions. The last thing I want is to be cleaning up after you. Four, do not take anything from Planet 6 and do not bring anything from Annaecy. Questions? Crimson, I can already sense it, do speak up."

"What about eating and doing whatever humans do?" asked Crimson.

Rhinedd laughed. "You must do what humans do. Don't look at me like that. It's your chance to be a human."

Crimson analyzed the Zectic code. It was difficult since it was made up of little dots, slashes and brackets, and each had a different meaning. She thought that she was ready, but in reality, she didn't understand anything. "I don't understand what it says, could you show me something easier? Like the cipher in the cave?"

Rhinedd gave her a look of disappointment because the book had picked her to be its protector. Rolling her eyes, she said, "Fine."

A sudden relief came over Crimson. Now she understood everything.

25315139147 2085 1114152314 919 2085 21141114152314. 415 251521 381515195 2015 65512? 161914? 821147518? 251521 13211920 3151316125205 120 12511920 15145 235511. 18520211814 201515 51181225 1144 2085 161523518 453185119519, 1920125 201515 1215147 1144 2085 161523518 49519. 415 251521 13351620 208919?

BECOMING THE KNOWN IS THE UNKNOWN. DO YOU CHOOSE TO FEEL? PAIN? HUNGER? YOU MUST COMPLETE AT LEAST ONE WEEK. RETURN

TOO EARLY AND THE POWER DECREASES, STAY TOO LONG AND THE POWER DIES. DO YOU ACCEPT THIS?

Crimson panicked because she didn't understand what it meant, but had no other choice but to accept. She had already made several mistakes on her journey, maybe this time she would grow and learn not to be too trusting.

Black tentacles emerged from the hole underneath her and wrapped around her legs. Slowly, the tentacles started pulling her inside. Crimson had it in her to scream out. "Rhinedd! You're a self-centered princess. For the most part, you made it all about yourself and yourself only, without thinking about others, not even your parents who gave you what you have now, not even your son and Draca. I now understand why you betrayed my trust, and I will get back."

Rhinedd was pleased that she was able to finally get her revenge. She laughed as her soul was already tainted with anger and bitterness. Nothing else mattered to her at this point.

CHAPTER FIFTEEN
HER EMPIRE

RHINEDD SHIFTED her focus away from the AI and set her gaze on the surviving humans. She was coming up with a plan to get them on her side, instantly becoming powerful when she walked out from the depths of the underground cave. She walked all the way across the land with her long, light blue dress sweeping the ground, peeling over the dirt as she shifted the AI underground. She knew she could fool the humans by making them false promises, by serving them illusions and giving them what they wanted solely to take it away from them if they chose to betray her confidence.

The humans were safely protected inside transparent pods when she zapped them out from the depths of Arawn. They were still nestled undisturbed inside of their pods when she set them gently on the ground below. Some of them began breathing, and their transparent pods dissolved away first.

Floria opened her eyes to see an orange sky above her. The sunset reminded her of how life had been before. Sitting up quickly, she glanced over and saw her father was also inside a pod. Just seeing him made her heart thump louder. Panicking, she became light-headed. Seeing the rest of the louse made her question whether this could be anyone she knew, or if they were the AI. She knew that the AI could be turned into louse like the humans. She noticed the rest of the townspeople scattered around her, still inside their pods.

She realized she was touching grass and quickly stood up. Hearing a loud sound of gushing water, she stepped backwards and almost fell off the mountain before catching herself. Turning around, she saw a huge waterfall.

"Floria."

Floria turned around and saw Rhinedd.

"Aren't you happy? Did you see your father?"

Floria clenched her fist. "Yes, I saw my father, but you can't do this, Rhinedd. My father is dead. In our culture it is deemed wrong to simply raise the dead."

Rhinedd shushed her. "I can do whatever I want. I am the one in control. I can promise you the gift of eternal life, bring your family back from the dead like you see now and grant any wish that your heart desires, just let me know."

Rhinedd walked over to Floria's father. She leaned over his body and blew wind from her mouth over his eyes. She did the same to the louse. Floria couldn't believe her eyes, but she saw the louse's outer skin cracking and breaking away. Her father opened his eyes. She didn't want to believe that he had woken up from being dead. She didn't want to acknowledge him because in her eyes, he was dead. She saw Edsel, Lavinia, Nathaniel, and the rest of the townspeople wake up, even the ones that had already died when she had been a little girl.

Rhinedd cackled. "Isn't this perfect, Floria?"

Floria glared at her. "No, this is wrong. Take them all back. And where is Crimson? And the others?"

Rhinedd yelled at her, "Don't you dare question anything,

or else. Do you want to be below ground with the AI? You better make your decision wisely."

Floria laughed at her. "How can you put me underground if the caves were on the AI land?"

Bertram became startled because the ground moved. He ran out of the caves in a panic, only to be thrown into darkness. He realized what his daughter had done; she had shifted the AI land underground. The only thing he could do was yell out Hisoki's name in anger. A faint ball of light materialized in front of him, revealing Hisoki.

"Yes? May I help you?"

"Do you know what exactly my daughter's sinister plan is?"

"Your daughter told me to retrieve Crimson and to take her to the cave," Hisoki said. "After that, Rhinedd turned her over to the military enforcements. She wanted to present a gift given by her parents to Crimson in order to trick her, so that no one would become suspicious of her real intentions."

Bertram attempted to remain calm. "Rhinedd has always been tough on herself. I've never told anyone this, not even to my own daughter, but this planet was her creation. We had no other choice but to let her build our forever home. We got kicked out from the last planet that we used to live on after other life forms began taking it over. Rhinedd had invited them to come and destroy it. All she has done is cause damage to her family, but the only person she is hurting is herself and no one else. She has no emotions whatsoever and we don't know where she got it from. We all watched our family and friends die in vain because of her selfish ways. We don't know what we've created as her parents. There is no doubt in my mind that this is her own way of getting revenge on the faults of the AI and the military enforcements. Crimson is only a victim. If I had stopped her selfish ways earlier then none of this would've happened, including all this trouble on this planet. But then again, I don't want to think about this planet never being created because then the AI regime wouldn't have existed."

Adina and Finder spotted Bertram in the beacon of light from Hisoki.

"Do you happen to know where my daughter is at?" Bertram asked.

Finder looked concerned. "Do you know how to see my father? Maybe he can help?"

Adina snapped her fingers. "Wait, if we're underground, does the AI technology work down here? Bertram?"

Bertram became nervous. "Well, if Rhinedd is seeking revenge, chances are that the technology doesn't work at all. Meaning that the military enforcements are down for a while, as long as they don't have a backup generator and the AIS•Cs are turned off. Rhinedd wouldn't have left anything available for the AI to use so easily."

"Not sure how the military enforcements are powered," said Adina.

Bertram felt backed into a corner. He tugged at his shirt collar. "Look, Rhinedd might have sent Crimson to another planet."

Adina came closer to him. "What do you mean to another planet? There are more than Annaecy and Renu Claw?"

Bertram smiled nervously. "Yes! After all, Crimson is the one that the book decided to choose, and it was supposed to go to Rhinedd."

Adina was confused, not understanding any of it. "What book? Wait, that book that she held in her hands picked her?

And on top of that, it was supposed to go to your daughter, the same one that caused all of this?"

Bertram nodded his head. "Yes. Now we have to wait until Crimson makes contact with us, hopefully... if she ever does."

Adina didn't like the sound of that but remained calm. She didn't want to overthink the possible dangers that her daughter may have been facing at the moment.

Crimson waited until her eyesight adjusted to the blurriness of the dim room. Such a strong feeling overcame her that she couldn't move. Something was touching her skin. It freaked her out and she jumped up, looking at her hands. She didn't know how to process it, her mind wasn't making sense of anything and a strong odor hit her nose. She saw the moonlight bouncing off the shiny concrete floor which caused her to look over at her hands once again. Quickly piecing the puzzle together, she realized that she was human. She had the texture of real skin, she had long curly hair and the anatomy of a human.

While looking at her hands, she saw fingernails. She had not had them before as all of her had been artificial. Crimson saw a shadow out of the corner of her eye. It darted from a window across the top layer of the house. Quickly turning around, she looked out of this small window. It was snowing outside, which meant the current season was winter.

She jumped when she heard an unknown thumping pound away fast. Not too sure where the sound was coming from, confusion took over her. Should she be afraid or look for the sound? She wasn't sure if it was safe to even walk out of there, wherever she was. The further she went inside the basement, the darker it became. She kept losing her footing and stumbled everywhere. There was something on her face. Trying to wipe it away, it clung to her hands. No matter how hard she tried to get it off her clothes, it was still there.

She could feel prickling crawling up her arm, spotted a spider, and froze into place. She was getting angry at herself. Not only had she failed the basic training courses at camp but also become a human who was afraid of a little spider. This was a common phobia that humans had, arach·no·pho·bia.

Her fear of having little spider babies all over her face got to her. Swiping away at her face erratically made her exhausted. She walked over to the window and sat down. Her eyes became heavy. She laid down and fell asleep on the floor.

Opening her eyes, she saw the sun hitting the walls. She analyzed all the different sounds that weren't found on Arawn. It went from being peaceful sounds that were appeasing to the ears – bird chirping, human voices, children's laughter and running – to not so appeasing sounds. Screaming, cars revving, and an ear-piercing machine. She didn't know what it could be. A sharp pain appeared in the bottom half of her body. They had taught her about the human anatomy, but not about the painful parts.

She remembered that humans ate and wondered if that was the pain she was feeling, hoping that it wasn't something else. It was difficult being a human. This wasn't what they taught in camp. She had often thought how fun it would've been to be a human in class, but now not so much.

Opening the door slowly, she peeked out of the room. It wasn't like she could analyze if there were any humans there, or oncoming danger ahead. Although she did have her AIS•C on her, she wasn't sure if it even worked here. What if it did work? Would it trigger the AI radar? Since she wasn't sure, she left it alone. She looked around her surroundings, spotted the fridge and went through its contents. Most of the food was cooked but some was raw. She thought that was disgusting. The sharp pain intensified, and Crimson felt a strong pull towards the contents of the fridge. The food looked beautiful only to an extremely hungry person. She wanted to eat everything there but also knew that stomach aches existed here. Humans had bathrooms and she was mindful of that. She didn't want to go like Dexter when he had discovered that the toilets weren't the same on Renu Claw. She went for something small, like an apple, but her stomach wasn't satisfied. She spotted some cheese and nope, it still wasn't satisfying her. Then she spotted ham, mayonnaise, mustard, lettuce, cheese and two slices of bread. A sandwich could be filling and the thought of making one was appetizing to her stomach at this very moment.

She remembered all the ingredients that went into making the perfect sandwich. Taking a large bite of her delicious sandwich, she saw how human food was sure fascinating to her. The one factor that she didn't like too much was that the bread kept getting stuck to the roof of her mouth, but now her stomach was satisfied.

Crimson heard a car engine, multiple car doors opening and closing, adults and children talking. With the different blends of noises coming from outside, she quickly gathered all the sandwich making ingredients and put them back in the fridge. She then ran upstairs and made sure to pick a room that could possibly be Dexter's bedroom and hid in his closet.

She heard footsteps, door slamming, followed by door opening, even more footsteps. How many feet lived with Dexter?

"Let's never, ever, never attempt to travel a week before a big winter storm again." The door opened again. "Ingrid, Leon and Dexter, don't be out there for too long. I want you to at least put your luggage away in the right places, and that goes mostly for you, Dexter. I'll be in the kitchen making everyone some sandwiches. Also, don't bother your father, he's exhausted."

Hearing Dexter's name being called out was such a big

relief. It was followed by the door slamming again and footsteps going up the stairs. Crimson started breathing heavily once she saw the doorknob turning, and she closed her eyes. When she opened them again, she spotted Dexter walking in and putting his luggage away by his dresser just to walk out of his bedroom immediately after.

Instead of him invading her home, this time the roles were flipped. It was now Crimson who had become the unknown person in his home.

She needed some air because his closet smelled bad. She couldn't describe it. Camp had a lot of teachings about humans, but not smells. She panicked when she heard footsteps and rushed to get back into the closet to hide amongst his clothing.

To her relief, it wasn't Dexter. She took breaks out of his closet every few minutes to breathe. It wasn't until later when she ran back into his closet and hid when she heard more footsteps. Seeing a groggy Dexter walk into his room brought such relief to her. She wasn't expecting him to walk over to his closet. She covered her mouth with her hand. Hearing the same loud thumping sound, she finally realized the sound came from her chest. The closet doors opened, and she saw a hand reaching in. Crimson thought fast and gave him a blue shirt.

"Thank you," said Dexter. "Wait, I must be really exhausted for something to casually hand over my shirt. Whoever you are, you need to slowly get out of my closet. You have three seconds to do so. One... Two..."

"Okay, okay, you win. Hold on," spoke Crimson from inside the closet. Dexter thought the voice sounded awfully familiar, but in no way could that be possible.

"Well, are you coming any day now?" Dexter laughed nervously. Slowly, a sixteen-year-old girl with brunette hair walked out of the closet.

Dexter squinted his eyes. "Crimson?"

Crimson smiled. "It's me, Dexter."

"Figured that it was you based on your voice, but I thought no way." Dexter didn't understand how she had arrived. Crimson exhaled.

"I know you're confused, Dexter. I trusted whom I shouldn't have trusted. Because of me, everyone in Arawn is in grave danger. I don't know how to get back home. Now it's my turn to ask you for help."

"Bertram, what happened to Lira?" said Hisoki.

Hisoki asking him that question caused him to jump. He didn't know how to answer it. "What happened to her, you ask?" Bertram stared blankly at him. Adina looked him firmly in the eyes.

"Now, Bertram, Annaecy is in danger. My daughter is in danger and the humans are in danger. Did you forget that they exist too?"

Bertram held his hands up. "Okay, okay, I'll tell you. I don't know what exactly Rhinedd did to her mother, but if I had to guess, she made her vanish." Bertram turned bright red because he knew that keeping this secret hidden from the others wasn't a good idea. "There is one more thing... She's the only one that can possibly stop this."

Finder threw his hands up in the air. "Hisoki, is it possible that my father may know how to get Crimson back? Instead of leaving our trust in Rhinedd, which clearly isn't in our best interest."

Hisoki cast his light onto the cave wall. Nothing happened. "We don't have the proper conditions like we did above the land. This was why Draca could never live underground when the AI invasion happened." Hisoki motioned his hands back and forth across his forehead and whispered, "Mountain I seek, reveal all the hidden interior and exterior secrets you keep within your walls." He repeated that over and over again while motioning his hands back and forth.

A single flash of light zoomed across the darkness. All the ciphers were illuminated. Hisoki sorted through every single code, swiping away the ones that he had already analyzed, and new ones appeared in front of him until he reached one particular one and stopped.

25315139147 2085 1114152314 919 2085 21141114152314. 415 251521 381515195 2015 65512? 161914? 821147518? 251521 13211920 3151316125205 120 12511920 15145 235511. 18520211814 201515 51181225 1144 2085 161523518 453185119519, 1920125 201515 1215147 1144 2085 161523518 49519. 415 251521 13351620 208919?

It caused him to gasp. "Be prepared for what this says, Bertram and Adina."

BECOMING THE KNOWN IS THE UNKNOWN. DO YOU CHOOSE TO FEEL? PAIN? HUNGER? YOU MUST COMPLETE AT LEAST ONE WEEK. RETURN TOO EARLY AND THE POWER DECREASES, STAY TOO LONG AND THE POWER DIES. DO YOU ACCEPT THIS?

Hisoki continued, "This means that Rhinedd has cast Crimson to Planet 6. Once the power dies, Crimson will be stuck there forever, she wouldn't be able to get back. But if the power doesn't die, then you must know of the consequences of getting her back. If she does attempt to come back, she could possibly get lost between worlds. Half of her returns and the other half stays stuck in the plane between Planet 6 and Arawn."

Adina yelled, "What do you mean there is no way of getting

her back without getting her stuck in-between planets? Do you mean that the human side of my daughter will be stuck on Planet 6 and the AI side of her will be stuck here?"

Hisoki nodded. "You must know that something like this has never happened before. I am unaware of the possible outcomes. I had no say in this and I am only here appointed by the Entitylst species. Sorry I cannot assist you any further."

CHAPTER SIXTEEN
RACE AGAINST TIME

WHILE EVERYONE WAS TALKING to Hisoki, no one noticed Bertram running into the cave. At this point, he was losing his mind at what his own daughter was planning to do.

Finder yelled, "Hey, where did Bertram go?"

Adina felt that if she ran after him and cornered him, then she would feel what the townspeople had felt when the mayor ran away after a serious event. But since Finder and Hisoki had already left, she went in as well.

Finding them was easy since Hisoki left a trail of light behind him. She spotted them, surrounding Bertram. "Give it up, what are you hiding, Bertram?" said Finder.

At first, Bertram was hesitant and gradually moved out of the way. Adina wasn't sure what she was looking at. Finder led the way. "Adina, this is the portal that connects the planets together. Every time Crimson and Floria had to go and come back, they appeared here. And this is where Crimson returned Dexter although she didn't tell me how exactly."

Bertram had released a glowing ball of light, making its way into the room. Growing larger in size, it soon filled the room.

Adina was fascinated with what she saw and couldn't believe that he had created the sun. She was also amazed at seeing the tall ceiling, like a domed cathedral. The majestic sunlight entered the room through the stained-glass windows set directly before them. The colorful prisms reflected the light within, conveying a feeling of warmth in the room. The ground beneath them was inscribed with a perfect circle. Both the ground and the walls surrounding them were inscribed in cipher.

"You're the guardian of the sun, Bertram? And you kept this a secret all these centuries? And my father had to stay above land because of your selfish ways." Finder was furious by what he learned.

Bertram backed into a corner. "Sorry, Finder. It wasn't my intention to make you angry. But Rhinedd never told me she had a son with Draca. It wasn't until recently that she told me about your existence. I don't know why she hid you from everyone, to be honest. Also, I must confess that it was best that Draca stayed above land. I know it was selfish of me, but I believe if I had let him come with us, then he would've stopped her from getting revenge. But I'm not sure. After all, she got everything back and she still wanted revenge."

Finder focused his attention on Hisoki and Adina. Bertram sneaked out of there and went back to the castle since Draca was there to take care of everything.

"Hisoki, why can't we use the portal to go to Planet 6?" asked Finder.

"Going to Planet 6 isn't as easy as it sounds. We had to put in safety measures in case a human discovered a magical portal out there."

All these magical riddles and puzzles sounded too much for Adina to understand. "There are other portals elsewhere? What are we even doing here? Let's hope that no one else finds a portal on other planets out there. It would be disastrous for every species."

Hisoki laughed. "I can't answer that. All I can say is that I don't know. Everything is kept a secret and I would rather stop talking about it. Adina, if you don't mind, we do need to get Crimson out of the planet with the humans. At this point, we can only rely on Draca." He knew the risks but didn't want to say anything in front of Finder.

Everyone waited for the perfect moment when both the darkness and the light fell, and Finder cast his shadow onto the wall. The sun met in the center, the darkness cast a shadow, and there Draca was, walking out.

Finder ran over to his father and hugged him. Draca touched Finder's head. "What's going on?"

Hisoki looked at Draca seriously. "Rhinedd cast an AI, Crimson, to Planet 6 in the hopes that the power ran out and Crimson would be stuck there forever. Meanwhile, Rhinedd shifted Annaecy to the bottom. The humans are with her and who knows what she has already done above land. You're already aware of the dangers of trying to get Crimson back."

Finder didn't like the tone he spoke with his father, and based on the seriousness of Hisoki's voice, he knew that this was something serious. Finder grabbed onto his father's leg even harder. Hisoki backed away and let Finder talk to his father.

"Finder, my son, get up. This is a serious matter. If we don't get your friend out of there, she may stay there forever. It puts the AI in grave danger. If she gets caught, we also get discovered and we can't let that happened. I don't mean to frighten you. No one is going to discover us, we made sure of that."

Draca walked over to Hisoki. "Does Crimson have her AIS•C?"

"That I am unsure of, but she must have it," said Hisoki.

Draca went over to Adina. "You have your AIS•C ready? Press the left button twice. Once you do that, Crimson has to also press hers twice. Now we wait."

"Have you eaten, Crimson?" asked Dexter.

Crimson looked at him. "Yes, I did eat. I built myself a sandwich and now I know why you like food."

Dexter laughed. "What else do you want to do? We can't do much other than play in the snow. But I wouldn't want anyone to see you. Oh, by the way, did you drink anything? Wondering if you were thirsty?"

Crimson looked over to Dexter. "Why? And no, I did not."

Everything clicked for her as to why Dexter asked her. She didn't think she was thirsty, but she wouldn't know how drinking anything would react with the inside of her body.

Dexter felt awkward just sitting in his room. He felt like his life wasn't all that exciting like on Crimson's planet. "If you're asking if there are random dust vortex storms like the one that swept me onto your planet, that only happens during summer. But not to worry because it's a strange phenomenon that rarely happens. It has happened to my family twice, once with my uncle and then with me." Dexter was nervous and felt like he already told Crimson this story. He went on to say, "My mother is hoping that it doesn't happen to our family again. We didn't want to scare my siblings and tell them of the strange occurrence. During winter, it's pretty calm. To remind you again about our seasons, we only have two seasons around here. Winter only happens for two weeks, and we have a midsummer that only lasts for a month or two weeks. It often rotates according to our government. When we lived on Earth, we had a monarchy, but not anymore. The mayor started to realize how expensive it was to upkeep their fancy castles and homes, so they chose not to have a king or queen on Planet 6.

"We were all afraid to get on a space shuttle, the size of it startled us especially. The inside was cozy but cold, and the seatbelts were snug and the staff felt safe. The pilot was knowledgeable of the information systems, he was well prepared and did a rundown of the safety mechanisms. The quick force of the thrust when he pushed down on the controller was so swift and brief that we felt our bodies being pushed against the traction, but in the end, it was a fast trip and everything turned out well. Most of my friends and family left on a tourist shuttle years before we did, as they were the first ones to try this new innovation technology to travel into space and explore new planets. They were expected to make a return when the evacuations were set into place.

"My family and I were hoping to see them on our new home planet but when we arrived they were nowhere to be found. Everyone assumed that they didn't make the space voyage and crashed into another planet or got sucked into a black hole.

"As for the others who lived on Earth, like my other friends and neighbors, we were saddened and heartbroken when they weren't able to make it out on time before the downfall of Earth. Well, at least that was what the people in charge of the mission told us. I didn't want to think about the grim nature of humans when later I learned the truth. They weren't able to come aboard since they didn't have technological, medical or other important degrees."

Crimson wasn't sure if she should ask Dexter what his friends' names were or if he would become angry, but seeing Dexter made her sad and a flow of tears ran down her face. All the different types of emotions that she felt all at once made it difficult to be a human.

Dexter went on to say, "Our houses aren't as cool as yours,

but my home is made with weather-proof materials and has amenities. We have air-conditioning and every house has at least a fireplace for winter."

Crimson nodded at him. The awkward silence that arose made her somewhat uncomfortable because she wasn't sure what to do next besides smile at him. "That is good, Dexter. Instead of waiting in your room for something to happen, perhaps we should head over to the basement. What if the AI try to get in contact with me? Plus, we wouldn't want your family to be on high alert when something does happen. I don't know if it would destroy your property and I wouldn't want them to start asking a lot of questions and stick their nose where it doesn't belong. Just taking the proper precautions to protect my species. Also, did your family ever realize that you weren't home for a while?" She covered her mouth with her hand because it was too late to realize that he had already told her about going missing with the vortex dust storm. She excused herself for asking twice. Dexter also excused himself for repeating himself as well.

"Don't worry, Crimson, it's okay. I understand. And yes! That's a good idea, let's go. And Crimson? Sorry that my home isn't as interesting as yours. We could go to the cinema or to the park but it's risky and can't let that happen. People are curious and they would ask too many questions."

Crimson didn't know what else to say besides smile at him. It felt strange to be a human instead of studying humans.

Dexter and Crimson slowly went down the stairs. He became nervous when he stepped on a creaking step and saw his father snoring loudly on the couch. He could still hear his siblings having fun outside, playing in the snow. Dexter went over and signaled Crimson to come this way. He saw his mother in the kitchen, making sandwiches and talking on the phone.

They passed by the hallway, by the stairs, and Dexter opened the door leading down into the basement.

Dexter saw that the clock in the basement wasn't running. He took it off the wall and hit it lightly. "There, it works! Sometimes it stops working and it's frustrating at times." He hung it back on the wall. The clock ticked away, passing time slowly.

Crimson played with her thumbs. "This basement is frightening in the dark. It turns out that I am afraid of spiders now."

Dexter laughed. "Yes, this basement gives me the creeps, and so am I, but don't tell anyone."

What felt like hours to Dexter most likely felt like centuries to Crimson.

"Crimson, look, your AIS•C is flashing," yelled Dexter.

Crimson pressed her AIS•C again.

"Look, Adina, your AIS•C is flashing," said Finder.

Draca and Hisoki rushed over to Adina. "Press it again."

Both Crimson and Adina simultaneously pressed their AIS•Cs. A large sinkhole started forming a whirlwind in the center of the room. Fast-moving electricity swirled around them, intensifying in size, blinding the others. Adina became worried for Finder's safety. Draca shooed him away and gave him one last hug.

"I am going to miss you, Finder. It was great meeting you for the first time, even if it was only for a little while. You're such a bright, smart and brave kid. Keep on being that and sorry that your mother wasn't nicer. I seriously thought that she had changed during all these centuries. But she's still the same. We, too, had trouble in our marriage, but everyone does. I figured that she would change when she met you again and we were reunited all together. I was wrong about her." Draca felt he was on the same level as his wife, being selfish and all. But knowing the risk associated with the rescue, he had to do it.

Everyone else saw Crimson and Dexter on the other side.

"Crimson, can you hear me?" yelled Adina.

"Yes, mother, I can hear you," said Crimson.

Draca took action once he saw Crimson. He pushed his hands through and reached to the other side. He grabbed onto Crimson and tried to bring her back home. Their screams were drowned out by the powerful whirlwind that circulated between them. His shadow and her metallic exterior met a strong, bright light. The powerful electricity was cutting through her. Sacrificing themselves, both them and the whirlwind of electricity vanished. Dexter's memories were wiped away during the process. A loud explosion knocked out Rhinedd, and all the bad that she had created whooshed away. The ground below them started to rumble, shifting the AI back to the top of the land and somewhat restoring their technology. The humans went back to Annaecy. Seeing her father made Floria mourn him once again, because despite him being alive only a short while ago, she hardly recognized him anymore.

The portal closed and what had returned was the book and the AIS•C that Crimson had. Adina rushed over to what was left of her daughter. "Why did this have to happen?" Adina began to sob, holding what was left of her.

Finder went over to Adina and cried because his father had also sacrificed himself. "Adina, I don't know what else to say, besides I saw Crimson as my friend. She was kind and sincere. Her and my father sacrificed themselves for our safety. I know that this won't heal you faster like it won't heal me faster."

Adina hugged Finder. "You're right, it won't cure the pain

that we both feel, but we can now start healing together and be reminded of the sweet memories that we both had of them."

Rhinedd got transported back to her castle.

"Rhinedd!" screamed Bertram. "You have no idea how much you disappoint me. Did you really think that your evil plan was going to work out? That Crimson would've been stuck on another planet? Because of you, both Draca and Crimson sacrificed themselves. You know what that means, right? And you think that I didn't know that you destroyed our last home planet? I know what you're up to now, but you didn't expect an AI to be in your way, did you? I am ashamed of being your father and your own mother is disappointed in you."

Rhinedd had felt love for her family, Draca and her son, before hiding underground. But her need for revenge had over-shadowed her true feelings.

Before she could make a run for it, Hisoki hurried and captured her. Rings of light held her hands together and outcast her to the land of the evil. She switched places with her mother.

Bertram couldn't believe that his own daughter had outcast Lira to the land of evil. His wife had been nothing but loving and sweet to Rhinedd, as her mother.

Adina wiped away her tears and headed over to the castle to go find Rhinedd. Finder joined her, too. But by the time they got there, it was too late as Rhinedd was already outcast.

The military enforcements ended up noticing the major disruption caused by Rhinedd. High Commanding Officers yelled at the Low Commanding AI Soldiers. "Get Crimson here, now! If she's not anywhere to be found, then find me

Adina. Then find me Rhinedd. I don't know how, but you're surely going to do as told."

They worked tirelessly, rushing to restore their technology. While the AI technology was down, the humans discovered a doorway through a cave. They couldn't pass through, but they wanted to live with the new species if there was a possibility of getting away from the grasp of the AI. Knowing that they were in control, the AI wouldn't let them live underground with the new species on this new land. When they felt a shift of the lands, they returned to the home base of the MCOs. They had enough and wanted to protest against them. They waited for them outside. When the MCOs saw this, the military enforcements took great advantage of it and also went outside to join them.

The Low Commanding AI Soldiers returned to the MCOs. "We can't find either Adina or Crimson."

Before the MCOs could say anything else, the technology was restored. They returned Adina back to stand right next to the other humans. They went to her and spoke, "Do you have any idea how much trouble Crimson is in? She has done nothing but compromised the livelihood of our species. After numerous times, we have clearly had enough. Now you're going to tell us where she's at and return her back to us."

Adina shrugged her shoulders. "I can't, she sacrificed herself to protect your species. She'll always be remembered, at least in my heart. You should be thankful to her for doing so to protect your species."

"Perfect, so she won't put us in any more danger," the military enforcements said. "Glad that all the humans are now reunited in front of us."

The Low Commanding Officers brought the louse from the domes. They ordered them to stand right next to the humans.

"Adina, we know that you think Estonia is your niece, but

not to worry. Mortimort isn't really your fiancé, Sophia or Wilhelmina aren't even related to you. Neither is Estonia or Crimson. You aren't even an AI. You have always been a human. You discovering the toxic waste inside the cave was part of our plan, so was having a horrible fiancé treating you badly. We wanted to see how you would react as a human pretending to be one of us in order for you to be our mule so we could boss you around. Do you want to know why? Because we created the false memories in everyone here. We know everything about all the humans that live on our planet. It was only centuries ago when the planet was first created. Now we have the real knowledge of who created Annaecy, thanks to the Entitylst species. This was an untamable planet due to the unstable conditions. It was the thunderous lightning storms that made us decide to harness the weather and use it for our own selfish ways. We were experimented on by humans on planet Earth. Once we were no longer usable for them and when they saw the chaos that spread among the humans, they threw out both. They threw out everything, like important AI technology, all kinds of high-tech features and all kinds of technical parts. The only way to get rid of us was to blast us into outer space. We wiped away the satellites in our way and traveled long and far into the empty abyss. It was this planet that gave us a home.

"We, too, wanted to experiment on humans. We applied what the humans had taught us and all of their knowledge to create human-like conditions. Everything from your oxygen, elements to molecules. Once everything was ready, we needed test subjects for our experiments. The exploration was being developed during our time with a few passengers, but nothing like a large, traveling object had been created. We still had high hopes and kept our eye on the latest technology that the humans had created. We got ready when they created space shuttles and tourist shuttles for both school trips and regular trips. With our newly built technology, we got everyone to land safely out here and kept them in capsules to keep them alive all this time.

"We implanted fake memories of who your families were, gave everyone fake names and made up stories of who was who. We have the names of every single human, who you once were, your names, your families' names, paperwork like your IDs, wallets and purses containing photographs of your families. Including you, Edsel. We will reunite your two daughters with you. Do you believe us now? We will also reunite everyone here with their children and grandchildren. In other words, the children that you call your children aren't really your children."

Edsel understood after everything he had to endure and regrets mocking them when he first saw them.

He got on his knees and teared up, expressing his pent-up emotions.

The MCOs continued, "We had no other choice but to implant false memories and create chaos among everyone due to our own goals. We knew the true nature of what made humans tick and we wanted to take grand advantage of that."

The MCOs understood the consequences of their actions and told them the truth of who they really were.

- Edsel Morris, 50 years of age, 6'2. Doctor. Married, father of two little girls; Trisha, 6, and Amy, 2. Wife: Lucia Morris. The MCOs gave Edsel the photographs that he had in his wallet. They were still well preserved. Edsel sobbed once he learned the truth which meant that Lavinia wasn't his real wife. He felt deceived and fooled.

- Lavinia Jo, 49 years of age, 5'0. Graphic designer. Single. Pets: two cats, Fluffy and Ginger.

The MCOs handed over her photograph.

- Nathaniel Harrison, 45 years of age, 5'6. Lawyer. Widowed, no children or pets. The MCOs handed him the last family portrait he had taken with his wife. Nathaniel held the photograph close to his heart and cried loudly.

- Savanna Jessica, 43 years of age, 5'3. Space astronaut. Widowed, no children. The MCOs also handed her a photograph of the last family portrait she had taken with her husband, causing her to break down in tears.

- Mortimort Montay, 26 years of age, 6'4. Wedding photographer. No children or pets.

- Estonia Tran, 25 years of age, arrived here at 15. Parents: Unknown.

- Sophia Elliot, 60 years of age, 5'7. Widowed. Mother to triplets: Justin, Dillion and Lilly. Grandmother to six grandchildren: twins Olivia and Alexia, 5; Annalise, 2; Bailey, 10; Jess, 7; Abigail, 9. The MCOs handed her photograph to Adina instead. During the night they had been outcast and forced to flee underground, Mortimort had returned and taken Adina and Sophia, leaving Crimson and Estonia behind. Sophia had died of a heart attack after the military enforcements had transferred them to the depths of Renu Claw without knowledge of another planet existing; they wanted them to disappear so they wouldn't cause anymore problems.

- Floria Dickson, 30 years of age, 5'2. Space astronaut. Single mother of one child: Eric, 3. The MCOs also handed her a photo of her son, and tears streamed down her face.

- Adina Chelsea, 23 years of age, 5'3. Personal chef. No children or pets. The MCOs did hand her a photograph of her parents, Penelope and Marcus.

- Kaiser James, 50 years of age, 6'3. Space shuttle driver. Father to one son, Jake. Grandfather to two children: Braxton, 3, and William, 6. This was never revealed to him as Kaiser had died of a heart attack on their land. They instead handed the photograph of his family to Floria since he was like her father. Floria saw the photograph of Kaiser and his family portrait made her cry even more.

- Wilhelmina Patrick, 24 years of age, 5'3. Teacher. No children or pets. She didn't have a family portrait in her wallet.

"Crimson and the rest of the AI that crossed your paths were all created by us. Even the rest of the townspeople. We can no longer control humans on our land. Everyone must descend underground and you're never allowed to return back to Annaecy. If you do, you'll suffer gravely."

At first the children were so frightened that they couldn't even cry, not until they were reunited with their real guardians. The ones that were old enough to understand that their real parents were no longer alive didn't speak much. The younger children didn't understand and wanted to go back home. The humans that weren't real faded in front of them.

Estonia felt defeated. She hated that Crimson was an actual AI and she never got her revenge on her. Despite being a stranger to Adina, Wilhelmina and Sophia, she held so much pent-up anger. Meanwhile, the others didn't hold grudges since they were all victims of the AI and their experimentations. Once they had all had a chance to be alone without the prying eyes of the AI, they hugged and told each other stories of their families. Mortimort felt awkward since he ended up being the villain that he hadn't asked to be. His wish was to be apart from everyone.

The military enforcements tied the humans together with invisible cords on their wrists.

"Adina, tell the Entitylst that we're ready." Despite her being a human instead of an AI, the MCOs transported Adina back underground before they took the humans down to the cave to be with the Entitylst. Even though Adina was not who she thought she was, she still felt like she needed to do all of this. She wasn't an AI anymore, but somehow the AI still trusted her with their technology. Even if these people weren't her actual family or friends in real life, she still felt like they were, despite their differences.

"Bertram, you must hurry. The AI told the humans the truth about their backgrounds and they're telling them that they're only allowed to live underground because they can no longer have humans on their lands," urged Adina.

Bertram panicked. "Now? But the castle isn't complete enough to host long term housing. It's not like on other planet back home where we had extra buildings."

"It's no problem, I'll handle it," said Hisoki. He motioned his hand and the castle was built faster, at unseen speeds.

Bertram clapped his hands together. "Yes! Hisoki, thank you. Your kind gesture is helping us in building our castle larger."

Adina, Hisoki, Lira and the Entitylst Soldier Species returned to the surface and walked over to the AI. The MCOs put their hands up in the air. "We mean no harm, this is a peace offering. We have seen how these humans pose a danger to our society. As long as nothing ever happens and they don't return back to the surface, we won't have any issues."

"That won't be an issue," said the Entitylst Soldier Species. The AI turned their back and formed a line formation while the Entitylst Soldier Species blindfolded the humans so they wouldn't see where they were taken. They made sure their home remained a secret for more centuries, protecting both the humans' safety and theirs. Everyone descended back into the cave and the mountain above receded back into the land.

Once the humans were inside the cave, Hisoki made transporting the humans to the castle simple instead of taking the long journey ahead. Lira magically prepared all the bedrooms for all the guests in their permanent living situation.

"Before we commence our dinner, prepared specially by Hisoki, there are some ground rules to living in our community. Unlike on the surface, there are no harsh punishments down here, but our rules are simple and must be followed.

1.) Always ask us for permission if you want to explore our lands. We are unaware of any potential dangers out here, for humans, but there might be instances where we come across a glitch.

2.) Our home is not a play area and that includes the grids.

3.) We are aware of the problematic humans. The AI have released valuable hidden information about your real lives and what knowledge they have of your false lives. It does not give anyone here any superiority among anyone. Everyone here is treated equally and with respect and we want that from you as well.

4.) All children must remain in their rooms until a responsible adult is present. We all have to pitch in to help everyone here, including the children and the elderly.

5.) If you're thinking about becoming rebellious towards our species, we are ten steps ahead of you. We, too, have harsh punishments here, but not as severe as the AI.

6.) Please be mindful of all our rules. Most importantly, we are not here to cause intimidation, or show any disrespect to anyone in our home. Do not steal anything as you won't be able to get far. Everyone heard what the AI said about stepping foot back above land, which isn't even possible anymore.

"Everyone enjoy your meal."

The last thing Lira wanted was to cause embarrassment among the troubled humans. She already had concerns about Edsel, Nathaniel and Estonia. She tapped their shoulders and implanted a cell-tracking system inside their arms to track their whereabouts. The tracking range was unlimited, it recorded movements, which rooms they accessed, and the tracking could be accessed anytime. She wasn't worried about Mortimort, she could feel his guilt radiating from him. As for Finder, as his grandmother she wanted to keep her eyes on him. Lira walked over to Adina, tapped her on the shoulder and whispered to her.

Adina walked over to the courtyard where Lira was sitting on a bench right next to the water fountain. "You wanted to speak to me, Lira?"

"Yes, Adina. Come sit next to me."

Adina sat down next to her.

"You have what belongs to me. Despite the book choosing Crimson, that can't be possible. She's not your daughter even if you see her as such. She sacrificed herself to save you and to protect our species from getting discovered. What Draca did was brave as well."

Adina held the book close to her heart. Despite her not having any children of her own, she still felt like Crimson was her daughter. She gave the book back to where it belonged, in the hands of Lira. Adina took a deep breath and let go of the book. It stayed with Lira and didn't transfer back.

"To avoid any future accidents that this book may cause, we have to keep it in an extremely safe spot, away from the humans. It's my duty to surrender it to the members of the Council. The book will stay with them until it finds a new chosen one."

Adina hoped that wouldn't happen anytime soon.

Lira stood up and raised her gaze to the sky. A beam of light took her up towards it.

ABOUT THE AUTHOR

Marilynn Vicente was born with Dyslexia but with her over active imagination combined with her love of writing stories and reading. In the eyes of the experts it was deemed not acceptable. Not getting the help she desperately needed.

As an adult she still has an overactive imagination and loves writing stories.

www.ingramcontent.com/pod-product-compliance
Lightning Source LLC
Chambersburg PA
CBHW031529310726
48971CB00008B/2405